# THE EDGE OF THE CIRCLE

# THE EDGE OF THE CIRCLE

CHRISTY KNOCKLEBY

Houseful of Chaos Press

# CONTENTS

# CHAPTER 1

# February 2nd: Hockey

There were eight of us playing a small, cramped version of hockey on an outdoor rink not quite large enough for the game. The snow fell in large wet flakes, that clumped together on our eyelashes, shoulders, and toques. The rink had been shoveled earlier in the day, but it would need to be shoveled again by morning.

I was having fun. The slight pinch of the skates was insignificant compared to the joy of getting a decent shot or stealing the puck away. A few of the girls on the ice were just there because of their boyfriends, and they weren't really trying. I tried. It didn't matter to me that most of the guys were part of the hockey league and significantly better at this than me. I was fast and determined. I did what I could and celebrated the small victories when they came.

Yet I couldn't help feeling that something was off. Were the others being a little too nice to me? I hadn't been body-checked into the snowbank yet. That was unusual. Those taking turns at the goal seem to have let shots of mine slip by purposely. Every so often someone started to say something only to be hushed by others. I didn't want to think about what it meant. I was pretty sure I knew. Mom had predicted this and urged me to stay home tonight. If it wasn't just my imagination, and people were treating me differently, then they were doing so because they'd hope to talk to me about tomorrow. They would want to have the talk everyone had been trying to have with me for months now. It was the talk that couldn't wait till tomorrow because tomorrow it would be too late.

I wondered if the inevitable conversation would come before the first person left. Maybe they would all want to talk to me together. I cringed inwardly at the thought. They wouldn't dare, would they? They must know I wasn't comfortable being the center of attention or having too many people talk at once.

I tried to force the fear away. I tried to focus on the puck. Still, I breathed a sigh of relief when people began to leave. Every person leaving was one less person I'd have to talk to about tomorrow.

"Good luck tomorrow, Jessica," Austin called as he left. I forced a smile and waved.

Ricky punched me gently on the shoulder. "You'll do the right thing, Jessica" he said.

A few others started untying skates, but there wasn't space for everyone on the bench. Joshua kept passing the puck to me and I kept tapping the puck back to him. Passing the puck gently wasn't much fun though, so I faked like I was going to go past him one direction and then pulled the puck back to me and shot around the other side of him to score on the empty net.

"Woot! Victory is mine!" I threw my hands in the air as though we weren't just fooling around.

"Make sure you talk to her," Martin called to Joshua from an open car window as he drove off. Now I knew I had been part wrong and part right. They had been treating me different, but not because they all wanted to talk to me. They wanted Joshua to talk to me on their behalf. That was okay. I could handle Joshua.

Soon Joshua's car was the only one left in the parking lot. We were alone. I threw myself down onto the snow-packed little bench, pulling my pink gloves off my hands and breathing warm air on my frozen fingers.

Joshua sat down beside me and took off his gloves. His gloves were thick ones with fluffy white fuzz on the inside. His hands felt warm when they wrapped around mine.

"You're freezing," he said. He lifted my hands up to his mouth and kissed them. "I'll warm you."

"I should have worn Luke's gloves. I thought about taking them when I couldn't find my good ones."

He leaned in to kiss me, but I pulled away. "Don't you have to have the talk with me?" If we were going to have the discussion, we might as well get it over.

"What talk?" he asked innocently. I raised my eyebrows and stared at him so he could see I was serious. No more stalling.

"Ok, we'll talk now," he said. "I promised the guys. Well, everyone really. You know what I promised. You've got to help protect Trevor."

"I'm not allowed to talk about any of this," I said. That was what the police officer had told me to say if anyone tried to talk to me about this. I had followed his instructions. I had used that line over and over in the months since the incident. I had said it to every member of the hockey team and to all my friends. Sometimes when I said I couldn't talk about it, people would try to have the conversation anyway. Then I would cover my ears with my hands and say, "la la la la" like my younger brother Luke did when my mom tried to talk to him about the birds and the bees. It didn't matter that I looked silly doing it. I had hung up the phone and deleted text messages unread countless times. I'd done everything I could to follow the rules the police had laid out.

"This isn't one of the rules I am comfortable breaking," I said to Joshua, but even as the words left my mouth I knew that tonight I'd have to talk at least a little. Joshua had promised our friends he'd talk to me. Even if it made me uncomfortable, I'd let him talk a little. I wanted him to be able to honour his promise.

Joshua brushed his hair out of his eyes. "Trevor has potential. He'll get a scholarship for hockey, but he can't have a criminal record. He'll lose the scholarship if he does. Don't wreck everything for him tomorrow," he pleaded.

I shook my head, sending bits of snow flying. "I don't have a choice."

Joshua wasn't going to accept that. "It's just a stupid sled. Henderson got it back and Trevor's family would probably have offered to pay for repairs if they could do so without worrying about Henderson pressing changes. There was no need to go to the police about it. He wouldn't have if he wasn't still angry over the septic tank."

We lived in Corsby, a very small town, and while for the most part the town was friendly enough there were certain little feuds that never seemed to go away. The McNickel family owned land right next to the Hendersons. As far as I understood the situation, a dispute had arisen years ago when it was found that the McNickel's septic system crossed over into the Hendersons' land. The McNickels hadn't been the ones to install the system. It had been there when they moved in. When the situation came to light, they had offered to purchase the extra land from the Hendersons. The two families never came to an agreement on the price, with old Mr. Henderson threatening to dig up the septic system if they didn't pay the price he demanded, and the McNickels insisting his price was outrageous.

The McNickels had since installed a new septic system in what used to be their yard, yet the hatred between the two families simmered. One family accused the other of trespassing to pick berries. Some of the fencing around Henderson's farm was sabotaged one night. The McNickels' apple trees had mysteriously been chopped down. There had been an escalating series of hostilities between the two families. Trevor stealing the Henderson's snowmobile and driving it into a pond was just one more chapter of their feud.

I hadn't wanted to be involved at all but what was I supposed to do? I could not lie to the police.

"I already made my statement to the police," I said. "I can't change it."

"There's got to be some wiggle room. You can change it

just a little. Please, Jess, please. Tell them you were mistaken. Tell them you can't remember when Trevor joined you on the road. Tell them you couldn't tell who was riding the snowmobile because the sun was in your eyes."

The sun hadn't been in my eyes, and I had watched Trevor walk right from where he tumbled off the snowmobile to the side of the road where he greeted Destiny, Mackenzie, Madison and me.

I shook my head again and began untying my skates.

"Tell them you were mistaken. Think of Trevor's mom. Mrs. McNickel is horrified about what this might mean to him. You should see her. Talk to her. It was just a mistake. It was a stupid mistake because he was angry and trying to show off." Mrs. McNickel was the school librarian. I liked her.

"I wasn't the only one there. I'm not the only one testifying tomorrow."

"Mackenzie, Destiny, Madison... they're testifying after you. If you say you never saw him out there, they'll back you up on it. They promised. *They* know how much this means to him."

Skates off, I jammed my feet into my boots and stood up. My heart sank at the thought of the others' willingness to lie. We hadn't talked about our testimony. I'd been firm about that, but I'd still felt like we were all in this together. We'd all say what happened that stupid day and it would all be over. We'd meet that night to laugh about it. It hadn't really sunk in that they might not be planning the same thing.

"Enough already," I said. "It's time to go home. Are you driving me or shall I walk?" The rink was only a few blocks from my house, but ordinarily Joshua would drive me home.

"Of course, I'll drive you. Why wouldn't I drive you?"

I shouldn't have asked. I should have just presumed. Now everything felt just a little more messed up, a little more awkward.

I tucked the puck into Joshua's pocket, glad for the excuse to get close to him. I flung my skates over my shoulders, so they hung by their laces. I passed Joshua his hockey stick and took my own.

"I can't do anything for Trevor," I said. "You know I can't."

We both threw our hockey sticks and skates in the back seat of his car. I climbed in pushing an old chocolate bar wrapper off the seat.

The drive home took just a minute or two. There were no stop lights in Corsby, and the one four-way stop was treated as a suggestion.

When we stopped in the driveway next to my house, Joshua leaned over to kiss me again. His lips lingered on my lower lip, warm and comfortable.

"Do the right thing," he said as he drew back from me. I was pretty sure we still disagreed over what that was.

Then he snatched one of my pink gloves. "Hostage," he said, "for you being community minded tomorrow."

*Community minded.* That was a joke. How could I be community minded in a place where petty feuds lingered for years? Why was it my job to be community minded?

The gloves were cheap grocery store gloves with nothing to recommend them other than their ability to be tucked away in a pocket when not needed, so I didn't protest the loss. I wished Joshua goodnight and shut the car door. He waited until I was inside to drive away.

The kitchen was bright and cheery. My parents were playing a board game with Luke. I listened for a few minutes as he argued with my parents. "Jessica gets to skip school tomorrow. Why can't I?"

"Jessica isn't skipping school for fun. She's legally obligated to attend court tomorrow."

"It will be educational," he pleaded.

"You can go instead of me," I suggested. It was tiring listening to him beg for something I dreaded.

I poured myself a glass of milk and headed upstairs. I'd had enough thinking about tomorrow without having to deal with the fuss that Luke was on the verge of starting.

"Don't forget to set your alarm," Mom called up the stairs after me. "You have to be at the courthouse early."

# CHAPTER 2

# February 3rd: Court

Being told to show up at the courtroom early must have been someone's idea of a cruel joke. I'd been waiting in a little room off the side of the courtroom for what seemed like hours. The judge was only in Corsby once a month, so every case was jammed into the same day.

Dad waited in the courtroom, keeping a seat saved for my mom. Mom waited with me in the side room.

"I'm surprised how many of your classmates are here," Mom said. "It seems half the high school is skipping today. I wonder how many are testifying."

I knew Mackenzie, Destiny, and Madison were scheduled to testify as well, but they must have found some place else to wait. I told Mom I wanted to go look for them, but she insisted I stay where I was. "This is where you were told to wait," she said, "and you'll be allowed to talk to them afterwards." That was her reminder that I wasn't supposed to talk to them about anything today.

"Mom, if we were going to talk about this we would have already. I told you, I've kept to the instructions and refused to discuss it." I felt guilty as I said that, thinking of last night's conversation with Joshua. I probably shouldn't have let that happen, but it wasn't like it had convinced me to change my story.

"Still, this is where you're supposed to wait."

So, I waited. I sat listening as people came and went whispering about different cases. A thin woman with bright red fingernails was debating dropping charges against a man who had hit her. Three men stood talking quietly about a disorderly conduct charge. I almost wished I had taken up smoking, just to have an excuse to leave the room every so often. The skirt Mom had insisted I wear stuck to the cracked vinyl covering of the seats. I bit my nails.

I debated taking another washroom break. I didn't need to use the toilet, but it would be a chance to wander for just a minute or two. I might be able to say hello to friends. I looked over at Mom. She was reading something on her cell phone.

"Mom, I'll be right back."

She looked up at me but didn't have time to speak.

"Jessica Cincinelli." A man in a suit stood at the doorway. "You'll be up in a minute."

My mom and I both stood up. She squeezed my shoulder and hurried from the room. I waited next to the man until gestured for me to enter the room and take the stand.

I sat down nervously, smoothing my skirt before looking up at the crowded courtroom. I could see Joshua standing at the back with his friend Pete, as though they had just walked in. When our eyes made contact, Joshua raised his hand, showing me the pink glove he was clutching.

The courtroom was crowded. Almost every bench was filled. The high school students filled the back third of the room, grouped together in little clusters. The parents that were present sat nearer the front. Mom had taken the seat Dad saved for her. They both smiled nervously at me. I forced myself to smile back at them before I let myself look at Trevor.

Trevor looked almost unrecognizable in a dark blue suit, but his hair was still loose and scraggly. He winked at me, then turned and whispered something to the girl sitting beside his father, in the row behind him. I was surprised it was Sasha sitting there. Last I had known, he was hooking up with Becky. I couldn't keep up with who he was involved with.

Trevor was the star of the junior hockey league, and that alone would have guaranteed him friends in our small town. He had other things going for him as well. Most of the guys in the school looked up to him, admiring his daredevil attitude. He was a bit of a flirt. Most of the high school girls have had a crush on him at some point or another, though my interest in him had been limited to a very brief crush back when I was in seventh grade. He had friends out of town too, and he would bring them to the bush parties to mix things up.

"Will you swear on the Bible or make an oath?" the clerk asked.

"The Bible," I answered. The question caught me off guard. I hadn't realized they would ask it. The Bible was standard, wasn't it? I'd go with that. I repeated the clerk's words.

The first questions were formalities. I had to state the day in question and where I had been. Then I was asked to tell the story. I closed my eyes briefly, picturing the day. Then I opened them and began to speak.

Destiny had said she needed our help convincing her parents that she couldn't drive the hand-me-down old rust bucket of a truck her brother had left behind when he left for university. She wanted something newer, something cleaner, less smelly and a lot less noisy for her daily drive into town.

"What are you going to do if you don't get something new," Madison had asked, "walk to school?" The school bus was always an option but not a remotely appealing one. Riding the bus meant an extra hour to and from school and limited one's ability for social contact. It was common for teens to start driving in on their own as soon as he or she earned a license.

That gave Destiny an idea. "I think I will walk. I'll show them I'm serious about never setting foot inside that truck."

She wanted us to walk with her to make sure the whole thing was doable. Mackenzie convinced her mom to drive her, Madison and I out to Destiny's house, so we could do the trial run on a Saturday.

We were all in good spirits when we started out. Mackenzie and I had worn snow pants, as unfashionable as they were. We all wore hats, gloves and scarves. It wasn't all that sunny out, but that was okay because the sunny days of winter tend to be the coldest. The weather was mild. We were together, laughing and talking.

We walked in the middle of the road, moving to the side when the occasional car needed to pass by us. The county plow had come through that morning and left behind a thin layer of packed snow, streaked brown with mud. Off to the side fields were sleeping under thick blankets of snow, interrupted only by the roads and the rows of trees used to break up the wind and protect the soil.

As we walked on we got colder, and we stopped joking quite as much. Destiny talked about the car she wanted to buy. Madison was worried about the English essay she had to write. Mackenzie filled in any silences with talk about her mother's new boyfriend. He was from Edmonton and only drove out on weekends.

The road between Destiny's family farm and the town seems short and flat when driving but walking we could feel all the little dips and hills. There were subtle valleys where we'd have to head down knowing that our legs were going to hurt as we walked up the other side.

Madison began to complain about the cold. "I'm not sure why we're doing this. It's cold out. Whose idea was this anyway?"

"Yours," Destiny said, "and I love it."

"It wasn't mine. I wouldn't have come up with this idea. This is crazy and if you do it on a school day you're going to have to get up so early in the morning. It isn't going to work. You're just going to have to try something else."

"It will work. It will work. You'll see. Besides, if I'm late for class it will prove my point. I need a car."

We were nearing Pearson's pond. Just beyond it was the golf course and then the school. We didn't have much further to walk but after the pond it would be all up hill.

"Look, over there." Mackenzie was the first to notice the snowmobiler in the distance. The snow was soft and powdery, so every time the snowmobile turned another cloud would shoot up into the air. I thought the driver was showing off, leaning back to make the front lift of the ground slightly as he shot back and forth.

"My fingers are getting cold. Let's keep walking," Madison said. Destiny had promised to buy us lattes at the coffee shop. No doubt Madison was already thinking of her caramel macchiato.

Destiny wasn't as eager to leave. "Just hold your horses, I want to watch this. I think I know who that is."

The snowmobile zigzagged towards us. Mackenzie and I looked at each other and shrugged. We were okay with waiting a few minutes.

The snowmobile slowed as it approached the pond, but did not stop. Instead the driver jumped off, rolling into a snowbank. The snowmobile continued driverless down the bank and onto the thin ice. It wobbled for a minute as the ice broke. The driver stood up, shaking the snow off and waving his arms in the air.

The snowmobiler came over to us and took off his helmet. It was Trevor McNichols. "Wasn't that awesome?"

He held his arms in the air and spun around, slowly, as though showing off for a huge audience.

"Are you insane? Why did you do that?" Destiny was almost squealing, her voice seemed so high. She'd had a crush on Trevor for ages and was normally a little giddy around him. Watching him sink a sled in the pond and walk away unharmed was more excitement than she could handle.

Mackenzie was calmer. "That sled is going to be so wrecked when you get it out."

"Don't worry about it," Trevor replied laughing.

"You can use my phone," Madison said, holding it out to him. "Call the police or a tow truck."

"Nah, Martin and I can tow it out with the tractor." Trevor grabbed Destiny's head and kissed her.

It was just a casual, celebratory kiss, but I rolled my eyes, thinking about how Destiny was going to never stop talking about Trevor now. I was happy for her too, because I knew how interested in him she was, and still confused why Trevor wasn't more concerned about his snowmobile. Maybe he was in shock at the whole thing. Shock could make people do weird things, right?

Trevor started walking towards town. Destiny stayed close to him and Madison followed, relieved that we had started moving again and would be getting someplace warm soon. Mackenzie looked back at the hole in the ice and then at me. I shrugged. If Trevor wasn't worried, why should we be?

"Come have coffee with us," Destiny was pleading as we entered town. She grabbed his arm as if to pull him along with her.

He freed himself easily. "I can't. Martin is waiting for me."

Destiny stuck her lower lip out in a pout and made a little huffing sound, but he wasn't swayed. Instead he turned back towards all of us.

"Hey, maybe don't mention the snowmobile, 'k? It wasn't mine and I'd rather it be a surprise when Old Man Henderson finds it."

Then he turned and jogged off past the school towards Martin's house.

"Didn't you think that was strange?" the lawyer asked after I had told my story.

"Yes, of course we thought it strange, but Trevor tended to show off in irresponsible ways," I said quickly. Then I bit my tongue. I had said to much. I knew I said too much.

Could I give examples of his showing off or being irresponsible? I didn't want to but since they asked, I answered. In seventh grade he had run across the flat roof of the school as a dare. Last year he had played chicken with the train after a bush party. I still remembered Madison screaming at him to get off the tracks. Those were two things I could think of that I had myself witnessed. There were other things that I had heard about but not witnessed. I didn't mention those. I knew I had already said too much. As I answered, I looked only at the lawyer's face, avoiding eye contact with anyone else in the room.

Did I know the snowmobile was his neighbour's snowmobile, and that he had taken it without permission? No, I didn't. I thought it was his family's snowmobile, and that if he was going to get in trouble for it, it would be with them.

Could I describe the snowmobile? It was white with green stripes.

Could I identify it in a picture? Yes.

Was I sure it was Trevor driving it? Absolutely.

Could the presence of a ski mask have confused me? No, not at all. He took the helmet and ski mask off when he joined us. He even kissed Destiny before we went off in different directions at the edge of town.

Was I certain about what had happened? I was.

After my testimony, the court took a break and Trevor

changed his plea to guilty. None of the other girls had to testify.

The pink glove was almost unrecognizable, lying in a puddle of mud outside the courthouse.

# CHAPTER 3

# February 4th: School

"Loser."

I heard the word hissed at me as I walked up the stairs to school the next day. Martin was a hockey player, one of Trevor's friends. I'd never been impressed with him. He had all of Trevor's carelessness with none of Trevor's charm. I ignored him and pushed through the big yellow doors of the long flat building that housed kindergarten to grade twelve. About twenty kids were clumped together talking in the foyer, but I didn't feel like interacting, so I just carried on through to my locker.

A torn piece of writing paper was taped to my locker with an abundance of packing tape. "Bitch," it said in dark black ink. I slid my house key under one side of the tape like a makeshift knife. Two or three students walked past me, echoing the sign as I worked. Once I had the sign down, I shoved it into the bottom of my backpack.

It could have been Trevor who put the sign up, but it

didn't seem like his style. Maybe Becky? The handwriting looked a bit like Destiny's, but she wouldn't do this to *me*, would she? Surely, she must have understood I had just done what I had to do. We were friends.

I had been starting at the floor as I wrestled with the possibility Destiny could do this to me, but I looked up when I heard Joshua's voice down the hall. I could always recognize his voice. He was standing next to Trevor. I saw them look towards me and then look away. It was not a good sign. I bit my lower lip and took a deep breath. Then as firmly as I could, I walked towards them. I might as well get this over with.

I looked directly into Trevor's face, as Mom always told Luke to do when he was apologizing to people. It felt awkward at the best of times. Today it felt completely wrong.

"Look, I'm sorry..." I said. I knew my voice didn't sound very apologetic. My apology was an attempt at following social norms; trying, after months of avoiding talking to him, to show him now that it was nothing personal. I had done what I had to do and nothing more.

Trevor didn't wait for me to finish speaking. He raised his middle fingers at me, both hands, and turned to walk away. Joshua hesitated for only the smallest second and then followed him.

"Joshua," I called. If he heard me, he didn't acknowledge it.

I have never understood before when people spoke of wanting the ground to swallow them up. The cliché made no sense. The ground had no throat, no stomach. How could it swallow a person? Yet seeing Joshua walk away, that was what I wanted. I wanted to be anywhere but where I was.

Joshua and I had only been dating for a couple of months,

but we had been friends long before that. Our mothers baby-sat for one another. We attended kindergarten together, and every grade since then. We played soccer together and wrote book reports together. There was the awkward time when we pretended a lack of interest in one another at school for fear of being teased about romance long before we could hold any real romantic interest in one another, but he'd visit with me at my house while our older brothers were hanging out together. In the winters, he was always busy with hockey, but he'd find time in his practice schedule to meet me at the outdoor rink. My aim with the hockey stick was much worse than his, and I couldn't keep up speed wise, but I had been determined to hold my own and we had fun together. How could he just walk away from me?

I put my head down, trying to hide the tears that were gathering, and I hurried into the English classroom.

Mr. Mercer, whose grey hair didn't quite cover the top of his round head, smiled at me sympathetically as I took my seat. Twice he stood up from his desk at the front of the room and made as if he was going to walk towards me, only to turn back.

I straightened the papers on my desk and began to doodle a collection of cubes, pretending no one else was there. My classmates began to drift in, but I didn't look up at them. I went over the lines again, darkening them, and then began to shade the faces of some of the cubes. No. This just prolonged the inevitable. I lay the pencil down, took a deep breath and leaned back in my seat so that I could watch as my classmates entered.

"Destiny," I said, forcing a smile as she entered. "That was some day yesterday, wasn't it?"

"I guess we know who our friends really are." She threw her nose into the air and looked away with the same dramatic flair she applied to everything in life.

I was learning who my friends really were.

Mr. Mercer let out a little squeak, stood up again, sat down again, and began rummaging in his desk. "That's it," he said, pulling out a small worn paperback and plopping it on his desk. He opened his laptop and set to work.

Becky and Mackenzie entered the classroom together. Becky looked away from me, but Mackenzie managed an awkward hello. Then she murmured something to Becky. Becky wished her luck and took her seat, while Mackenzie crouched down next to my desk to talk.

"Look, about next Friday," she said. She was speaking twice her normal speed, but I knew what she was going to say before she finished. "You can't come. I'd like you to be there, but you understand, no one else will come if you do, right?"

"Mack..."

"They say you'll report them. For drinking, you know. Most of us aren't legal age yet and there could be other stuff."

"Mackenzie, I've been at parties before. You know I don't report what happens."

She looked down at the books in her arms, avoiding eye contact. "You can't come," she repeated softly, and then stood up and hurried away. I listened to the clunk as her books fell on the top of her desk.

"Class will begin now," Mr. Mercer said. He held the worn paper back up in the air. "We're going to move up our

Shakespeare play and start it today. I'll put the text on the screen, and I'll need a few volunteers to read lines. We're looking at *King Lear* this year." He paused and laughed at his little rhyme. When he realized no one else was going to laugh too, he busied himself starting the PowerPoint.

There were whispers around the room as people shifted in their seats. Martin, sitting behind me, leaned far back and put his feet up on my desk, pushing me to one side. I shoved back, forcing his feet off the ground. His desk rattled as he regained his balance. Mr. Mercer looked up. He gave up on getting the PowerPoint started and stood up with the book again.

"*King Lear* is about a king who asked his daughters to say something they shouldn't have had to say. One of his daughters knew that the answer the king wanted was a lie. She could have said that lie. The king would have loved her more for it and given her the best share of his kingdom. However, she was unwilling to do so. She told the truth. Very courageously, I might add, but the king was humiliated by her honesty and punished her. As a result, his whole kingdom fell apart."

So that was it. English class was about to become a sermon in my defense. I could feel my classmates' hatred. I put my head down on my desk. A dark cloud had completely engulfed me. I was cut off from everyone and rejected by my classmates in a town where I would be stuck with the same twenty kids my whole school career.

My social life was over. My Friday evenings were open now. Mackenzie would have her party and there would be other parties after that, but I wouldn't be invited to any of them. My parents would be happy. They didn't approve of partying. They were always worried about what I did in my spare time. That was unfair of me. They cared, which was good, because I was going to be spending a lot more time at home with them if no one else would talk to me.

Mom must have known what my day would be like, because she left work early to be home when Luke and I arrived home. The look on my face stopped her from asking how my day went. Instead she just poured a glass of milk and set a bag of cookies on the kitchen table.

After a couple of cookies, I started telling my story. I wasn't more than a few details in when Luke started getting upset.

"It's not fair," he whined.

"Life is unfair," I said. "That's what I'm saying. None of this is fair. I didn't have the slightest choice, but everyone acted like I somehow chose this. Like I wanted to rat Trevor out."

He persisted, his voice getting louder. "It's not fair. The teachers should stop them from being mean to you. The teachers should insist they be nice. There should be signs on Trevor's locker saying what a total loser he is. Loser! Losers like him shouldn't be allowed to wreck things for the rest of us." He was almost yelling and in another minute or two he would be out of control. Luke was autistic and had trouble calming himself when he started to get upset. Mom would need to spend the next hour calming him down. Her attention was lost to me.

I took my cookies and milk and retreated to my bedroom. My cat followed me up, meowing as I opened my laptop.

As soon as I logged onto Facebook, I knew doing so was a mistake. "You lying, good for nothing, whore," one private message began. It was from a guy a year above me in school. In grade eight he'd told me how good my butt looked through my jeans, and I'd avoided being around him ever since. His Facebook account was easy to block. Harder to deal with were the messages from friends. Destiny had tagged me in a picture. It was a selfie she, Mackenzie, Madison, and I had taken together at her Christmas party. She had used photoshop to cut my image out of it. There was just a big white empty space where I had once been smiling.

My throat clenched up. I slammed my laptop shut. After a minute or two I opened it again. Turning it off wouldn't help. I had to change my Facebook settings to private and un-friended everyone who wrote to tell me what an awful person I am. Soon I had just a handful of cousins and aunts on my feed, all from out of town.

"I guess I'll be wasting less time online," I whispered to the empty room.

I cried myself to sleep that night.

# CHAPTER 4

# February 5th – 10th: Pepper Spray

The second day was no better than the first.

A new sign had been stuck to my locker, this time with some sort of glue. I scraped at it for a few minutes with my fingertips before giving up. It said "Bitch," and I angrily added "Yeah, so what?" in red pen. Then I leaned my head against the locker door while fighting back tears.

Later I cornered Mackenzie at her locker. "What was I supposed to do? What were *you* planning on testifying?"

"I don't know," she whispered but then turned and hurried down the hall. Destiny and Becky glared angrily at me before they caught up with her and linked arms. I thought Mackenzie's backward glance was kind of sympathetic, but when I tried phoning her house that night she wouldn't answer.

Next to Joshua, it was the loss of Mackenzie that hurt the most. We'd been inseparable for years. Mackenzie had moved into town when I was only seven years old. We had met at summer camp, and then she started school with me during the fall. She'd always been the strong one in our group. She would be the one to take the lead in class projects, deciding who would do what so that everything got done in time. She'd held Madison and Destiny together when they argued over guys. I pictured her like a strong wooden fence post set deep in the ground - the kind that can have barbed wire pulled taut against it but still stand firm. The wire was pulled too tight this time, the pressure too great. Or maybe this was her way of dealing with the pressure – block out one person, so that the rest of the group could stay together.

On the third day someone scraped their key along my dad's car. When Dad saw it, he phoned his friend at the police station, an officer named Johnson. The two of them went out for a beer that night.

The next morning, as I was putting my coat and boots on, Dad gave me a small container of bear spray. "Keep this," he said. "I don't want Trevor coming near you when you're alone, okay?"

I gulped and nodded. The implications of what he was saying were terrifying. What had I gotten myself into? This wasn't how things were supposed to be going. Still, I took the container from him and I turned the container over in my hands. It was small, about three inches in height with a black button on it.

"Where did you get this?"

"Johnson had an extra from his last camping trip."

"Do you really think I'll need it?" I asked. I started at his face, trying to assess how nervous he felt, that he would give this to me.

"Read the instructions. Memorize how to use it. Then tuck it away in your pocket just in case."

The details of how to use it where in white ink on a black label. The instructions said to be sure one was upwind from the target. How one was supposed to be sure of that with either a bear or a human? I tried to picture myself holding the canister out and spraying it at Trevor. I couldn't quite picture that. I'd probably bungle it or let him grab it away from me before I sprayed it. Probably it wouldn't be any help.

I put the canister on the shelf above the coat hooks, but Dad took it down and put it in my coat pocket.

"Just in case," he said.

The third and fourth days continued much the same as the first two. In the hallways, I tried to linger within earshot of the teachers, hoping their presence would stave off the worst of the comments. To my disappointment even standing next to a teacher didn't prevent classmates from calling me a whore. The teacher ignored it. A few teachers were openly hostile to me. I avoided the school library. I didn't want to face Trevor's mom.

I hoped after a weekend that things would die down a bit, but they didn't. On Monday I had just settled myself comfortably in my seat for math class when Martin bumped hard into my desk. My pencil flew out of my hand and was kicked across the room. I stood up and walked over to where it landed. When I bent down to pick it up a heavy boot crushed against my fingers.

"What did you do that for?" I said, pushing the person to the side. It was another hockey player.  I grabbed the pencil and went back to my seat. My hand was still aching when the math teacher, Ms. Evans, had entered the room.

Ms. Evans had short reddish-gold hair that changed colour slightly depending on how close to the window she stood. She wore tight jeans and a slightly oversized shirt. I'm sure she had at least an inkling of the sexual comments the students frequently made about her behind her back, but she never let on that she heard any of it. Instead she always focused on the math.

"Pencils and paper out please. No, you won't need a calculator today, Austin." The calculator was probably the least used app on any of our phones, but that was her standard rebuke to anyone whose phone was visible.

I debated, just for a moment, asking to leave the room, maybe to find some ice for my hand. Did I want them to know how badly hurt I was? I didn't. I forced my hand to curl around my pencil, ready to copy down the equations she was about to give us.

The fire alarm went off during second period, interrupting Mr. Mercer's lecture on the significance of storm clouds in Shakespeare's plays. We all had to evacuate the school. We had to check in with our homeroom teachers first, but after that no one really paid much attention to the high school students. We were supposed to just stand there shivering, but some of the students wandered off; a few were noticed by the teachers and called back, but I suspected some succeeded in ditching school entirely. Trevor and Martin were both gone by the time I thought to look for them.

I had been cold that morning, so I had worn my coat into the classroom. I was glad of that. I was luckier than most of my classmates. Destiny had three layers of shirts on but none of them covered her arms. She had her arms crossed trying to conserve warmth. I saw Mackenzie talking to her. I suspected Mackenzie was probably offering to lend Destiny her sweater – Mackenzie would have long sleeves on underneath – but of course Destiny would refuse. Madison was doing jumping jacks.

I turned around, looking through the crowd of mingling teens. Joshua was wearing an orange hoodie, his hands tucked inside the front pocket. He looked cold, even with the fleece hood over his head. Part of me wanted to go stand beside him and try to warm him up with a hug. I imagined different ways he might react if I did that; none of them would have been good. I hadn't approached him since the first day after the trial, and he'd stayed away from me since then. I thought he might have had the courage to at least phone or texted or in some other way attempt to communicate privately, but he hadn't.

I looked down at a chunk of dirty ice that would have fallen from some car earlier. I stepped on it, measuring how much of my weight it took to crush it. Then I walked over to the edge of the parking lot, to pick up some clean snow. The snow felt good against my hand. I thought there might be bruises forming.

It felt strange being on my own. Every fire drill before I

would have stood with friends, joking or complaining. Standing alone still felt unnatural, so I decided to go check on Luke.

The elementary students were lined up in the teachers' parking lot in tight supervised groups. Most of the kids were visiting with their neighbours. Luke was bobbing up and down on his toes. The other students gave him extra space; I suspected it was to avoid him bumping them.

"Luke," I called, as I got close. His classmates turned to look. His teacher smiled at me. I wasn't supposed to be there, but I didn't think she minded. She knew Luke sometimes needed a bit of extra help. "Luke, are you okay?"

He stopped bobbing. "The fire trucks aren't here yet."

"It's probably just a drill," I said.

He shook his head. "It's too slow for a drill. It's too cold."

That was when the police cars showed up. The younger kids all got excited, pointing at the car as the officers got out and walked into the school. Luke looked smug. He was pleased with himself that he had known it was not a drill.

"Look, Luke, I've got to go back to stand with my classmates."

He nodded and began to bob up and down again.

I hurried back over towards the high school students. I wasn't quite sure where to stand. I didn't want to look as alone as I felt, but I didn't want to get too close to people I wasn't welcome with either. I positioned myself on the edge of the crowd and started counting silently to myself. I had gotten to 3198 when we were let back into the building. Two police cars had come, but no fire trucks.

By lunchtime rumor was spreading about what the morning's disturbance had been. I was in the washroom when I heard what happened. Two people were talking at the sink, while I was in the stall.

"Can you believe it?" I overheard an eleventh grader saying to her classmate. "Someone was carrying pepper spray!"

"What happened?" the classmate asked.

"Ms. Evans saw something under one of the desks and reached to pick it up, and the spray went off. The whole classroom had to be evacuated and I guess someone pulled the fire alarm. The firemen called the police. Is pepper spray even legal?"

"I wonder whose it was. Imagine thinking one would need it here! This isn't the city. No one needs it here." The two girls left the washroom.

My hand went to my jean pocket. Empty. I left my stall, washed my hands and walked quickly to my locker. I had worn my coat in class that morning. I checked the coat pocket. Empty. It was empty. It had been my pepper spray that Ms. Evans had found.

I didn't think I would be in any trouble legally for having had the pepper spray. It had been a police officer who had suggested it to my dad. Still, I was nervous about it. I didn't necessarily want anyone to know it was me who dropped it, but I didn't want to feel like I was trying to keep it a secret either.

I found Ms. Evans leaving the principal's office. "Ms. Evans, can I speak to you a moment? Privately?"

"Oh dear," she sighed, looking at me, "Look, I know things have been tough for you this week, but I really can't..."

It took me a minute to realize she was worried I was

coming to her for help with my social life. "It's not about that," I said. "Please?"

"Very well." We walked in silence back to her classroom, her leading and I following a few steps behind.

The room was freezing. There was a large fan in the room and the windows had been propped open.

"It was my pepper spray," I blurted out. "I'm sorry it fell out of my pocket."

"Yours?" she said, leaning back against her desk instead of walking around to take a seat.

"My dad gave it to me."

"I believe the police have it now."

"That's okay," I said. "I don't need it back. I just wanted you to know it was me."

"Thank you for coming to tell me."

I turned to leave the room. Lunchtime would be almost over, and I hadn't eaten yet. If I hurried, I would still have time to wolf my sandwich down before French class.

"Jessica."

I turned back to Ms. Evans.

"I'm sorry everyone's giving you a hard time. If I knew what to do about it, I would, but I'm afraid if I try talking about it, I'll just make things worse for you. But if you're scared enough you need to carry pepper spray..." she let that thought trail off.

"I'm not scared," I said, wishing that were true.

For the rest of the day, I thought about what Ms. Evans had said. Was I scared? Dad was probably overreacting with the pepper spray. That probably hadn't been necessary, but the fact he had given it to me was alarming. He was scared enough to think I needed it. I wouldn't, would I? People might be nasty, but they wouldn't hurt me, would they?

The aching in my fingers assured me that yes, my classmates were not above hurting me. Martin wasn't, at least. Maybe Trevor. Who knows who else might?

It didn't make sense for me to go to school, just to sit there day after day in fear. There had to be an alternative.

"I'll drop out," I said to myself. No, I couldn't do that. University was a year and a half away, but it was still my goal. It was how I intended to escape the town. Dropping out wasn't an option.

I'll do online courses or something. I had seen a video online talking about teens who studied at home. There were all kind of possibilities. I knew my mom wouldn't do anything too labour intensive on her part, but supposedly there were online classes one could attend right from home. The thought of staying home made me hopeful. I turned the idea over in my mind as I waited out the afternoon classes.

"I'm not going back," I announced at supper after Luke had recounted the adventures of the fire alarm going off. "I'm never going back there."

"Surely if you talk to them..." my mom started. She let her voice trail off. There was a moment of silence before she started again. "Mackenzie? Joshua? I could speak to Joshua's mom?"

"No Mom, you can't." I said. I wasn't five years old. Mom couldn't arrange play dates for me anymore. Besides, she'd probably already talked to Joshua's mom and Mackenzie's mom. It didn't matter that the parents could be reasonable about things. We had a world of our own.

"Maybe Chad could talk to them?" she continued. Chad was my older brother. He was off at university, studying chemistry. He returned every month or so for a visit, sometimes timing the visits so he could come to a bush party and hang out with old friends.

I tried to picture Chad talking to people for me. He kept in touch with Martin's sister and Madison's older brother. He knew most of the kids on the hockey league. But the momentary hopefulness flickered away. I couldn't quite picture him coming to my aid on this. What could he say? If he had social capital it was because he knew not to waste credibility fighting for lost causes, and, at the moment, I was a lost cause.

My mom came put her fork down and reached over to brushing some hair back behind my ear. "Homeschooling could work. You could do that, but won't you be lonely?"

My dad smiled. "We can build a little schoolroom in the attic and you wouldn't ever have to leave it again. You can live up there till you're sixty." I knew he was thinking of one of his Sherlock Holmes episodes. It wasn't in the new one with the handsome Sherlock, but in the older series with an episode where a man locks his step-daughter away, so she can't get married and take her inheritance away from him. I didn't have any inheritance coming, but my dad didn't need that incentive; he would willingly lock me away if he thought it would keep me young and innocent.

"Till university," I said. "You can lock me up till university. Then I can leave this godforsaken town."

"I'll call the secretary at the school," my mom said. "She'll know how I can sign you up for online courses. You know I work though, so I won't be able to help you much. Let's see. I could probably come home early Wednesday afternoons, and we could go over your work together. You would have to show you were making progress on your own." My mom was nothing if not practical. "But are you sure this is what you want?"

"Yes, it's what I want. I'm not going back there," I said.

# CHAPTER 5

# February, but particularly February 27th: Luke

For almost as long as I could remember, I had the image in my head a circle of people surrounding me, loving and supporting me. Back when Luke was a baby and mom was suffering from depression, I had felt scared and alone a lot. Mom had taken a couple years off work and was home with Chad, Luke and I, but she also wasn't there. She was off in her own nightmare. She'd hold Luke with one hand and slap peanut butter sandwiches down on the table for Chad and I, and all the while she'd be mumbling "sorry, sorry, sorry...". I'd ask what she was sorry for, and she'd say it was nothing, just memories of little mistakes she'd made long ago. Chad would go play computer games, and I'd sit playing alone in my room. When my mom was feeling alright, and the depression was cleared enough for her to think, she'd come and sit with me, and she'd hug me and tell me everything was alright.

"Don't be sad," I'd say.

"Oh honey, I wish I wasn't."

"I don't want to be alone," I'd say.

Then she'd tell me I was never really alone. I had a circle of people caring for me, even when they weren't in the same room. She and dad cared, and Chad, even though he spent as little time at home as he could manage, and baby Luke. My teachers cared for me too, even when I wasn't in their classrooms. My friends were part of the circle too – Mackenzie and Joshua, and later Destiny and Madison. Their families were part of it too.

Over time the depression lifted. Mom started cooking real meals again instead of making sandwiches and heating up frozen dinners. Her smiles playing peek-a-boo with Luke grew less forced. I remember the first time after Luke's birth that she really laughed. Luke was a year or two old. I had just gotten home from school and we were having an afternoon snack. Mom had put crackers and cheese and sliced apples on the table and Luke grabbed for some, claiming it as "yours" while he did it. He meant the apple slices were his, but we always said "yours" as we gave him things, so he thought that was what the word meant. His.

"Mine," I said taking an apple slice for myself. "Mine" Luke repeated, handing me a cracker. Clearly, he thought "mine" meant anyone else's things. We spent the next half hour passing things around trying to help him see that "yours" could refer to anyone's things except the person speaking and "mine" referred to what belonged to the one speaking. Mom laughed, and I laughed too. After that I knew mom was going to be okay.

Even when mom was better, I had been glad for my circle, glad for the others I could turn to for help. Mackenzie, Destiny and Madison where never more than a phone call away. Mackenzie helped Destiny on her homework. We all helped Madison with her fears and anxiety. I helped Mackenzie, listening to her troubles when her parents got divorced. She listened to all my complaints about my family. And Joshua – Joshua had always been there to make me laugh, both before and after we started dating. I was safe knowing there were people I could turn to when I needed them.

Now it felt like the circle was gone. My friends had abandoned me. All that was left was my own family - Mom and Dad, Luke and Chad, though my relationship with Chad was strained at times. I had just three or four people. It wasn't enough to be a circle around me. Mom and Dad had their work, and they had Luke to care for, with all his special needs. I knew they all cared, but caring wasn't enough. I was on my own really.

The online courses were easy. Starting in the middle of a semester I didn't have an option for live online classes. Instead I would work through little modules on my own, emailing assignments to a teacher in another city. Mom bought me a day planner and I wrote out what my goals would be. As long as I could show my mom a list of goals and that I was regularly crossing them out, she didn't take much interest in the details.

I never got a schoolroom in the attic, but I sat with a laptop in the living-room most of the day. My cat, Sandy, took my laptop as a challenge. She was always trying to position herself on the keyboard and keep me from doing my work, but I would simply move her, time after time, onto the cushion next to me.

Math was the only subject I had a proper old-style textbook for, and I had to check all my own answers from the answer key. My only contact with my math teacher would be during unit tests. I was fine with that though. Math was my strong suit.

When I finished my work for the day I would go for walks, wandering around the town. Occasionally on my wandering I would see a classmate. Sometimes I would try to say hello, but whomever it was would pretend he or she didn't see or hear. Sometimes I just turned and walked the other direction. I was worried some that I might run into Trevor or Martin, but they tended to drive, rather than walk, so the chances of running into them were limited.

I started preparing supper more often. It gave me an excuse to buy groceries, which gave me an excuse to talk just for a minute about the weather or the price of fruit with whomever was at the till. Also, I liked feeling useful. It was my way of thanking Mom and Dad for letting me stay home.

Sometimes I went to the grocery store late in the day, when Luke was out of school, and I could drag him to the grocery store with me. Then I had company on the walk. He always wanted to split a chocolate bar on the way home. Normally about five minutes into the walk I'd regret taking him with me. Luke wasn't very good at listening to other people talk about their interests. Most of the time he wanted to talk about

Minecraft. I learned all about zombies, skeletons and how to make little electrical type things out of a type of material he called redstone.

"In Minecraft," he'd begin, "you can fly faster if you hold a firework rocket while gliding with an Elytra."

Sometimes I would just nod and make reassuring noises, but sometimes I'd try to join in. "Elytras are those wing things, right?"

I only had so much patience for talking about Minecraft, so I tried my best to get him to talk about school. I was desperate for news about school. A few of Luke's classmates had older siblings. Maybe I could get a little bit of the gossip. I wasn't entirely sure I wanted it, but I couldn't resist either. Gossip wasn't Luke's strong point though.

"You know what I hate?" He began. "I hate it when we're standing in line and someone says that he'll let someone else into the line ahead of him in exchange for the other person letting him in front of him."

It took me a bit to parse what he was saying.

"It's a way of cutting in line," he argued.

That I could understand. "I hated that too, when I was in school."

"Ben does it all the time." Luke continued. "And when I talked to him, he pushed me."

I'd heard quite a few stories about Ben. "Did you talk to your teacher?"

"She says I have to be more patient with Ben. She went on about how patient and helpful Ben is to other people and how I just need to get to know him more and not get upset.

That's not fair. What does it matter how nice he is to other people if he's mean to me?"

I could agree with that.

We were approaching the store. "Will you be okay to come in?" I asked. He shook his head, so I left him in the parking lot while I grabbed the groceries. When I came back outside he was still thinking about how unfair some people are.

"I hate Ben," he announced.

"Don't hate Ben," I said. It was a reflex on my part. Hating people was wrong.

"Why? Don't you hate Trevor? Or Joshua? Or Mackenzie? Isn't that why you cry at night?"

I hadn't realized he had heard me crying.

"I don't hate them," I said. This was a lie, of course. I did hate them, but I couldn't share that with my younger brother. I was supposed to be the good example.

"Trevor is not all bad. Look at how he plays hockey or how generous he is with his friends." I didn't add that his generosity often involved illegal substances. I couldn't believe it had come to this, that I was trying to defend him, but I didn't want Luke hating people. Particularly not people in town. It wouldn't help his social life to go around blurting things out about hating people.

Luke wasn't going to get lured into my thought patterns though. He has his own. "So? What does all that good matter when he asked you to lie for him and then turned everyone against you when you didn't?"

"It was wrong of him," I said measuring my words carefully, "but one, or even a few bad deeds, don't outweigh the good."

"Well then a few good deeds can't possibly outweigh the bad!"

"It's okay, it's okay," I murmured, hoping to sooth him. I cast around in my mind for some other topic I might be able to get him interested in. "Don't be angry."

"I have to be angry. You're never angry enough. You should hate him. You can't say that one bad action didn't override the good when that's how they treated you. They act like your one action overrides everything else. They're not being fair to you, so why do you have to be fair to them? It's not fair."

His mind jumps quickly through related topics. I've always been in awe of him for that.

"Look, it's like when the teacher told me I have to care how Ben is to others. Why does that matter? Why should it matter at all to me? Why should we say our own thoughts are irrelevant? Why should we have to degrade ourselves in order to try to maintain some belief that they are good people? It's not fair."

He was getting really upset. His shoulders rose. His head pushed forwards and down. I had years of experience watching him get angry and I knew it was important I calm him down before he starts yelling in the streets.

Luke was like a force of nature, the voice of all injustice in the world. What the rest of us kept hidden he would scream out to everyone. Those things we all had to learn to accept he would rage and fight against. Mom and his therapist were continually working to help him find ways of containing the noise, crying in private with someone he trusts rather than melting down in the grocery store or on the street.

I spent the rest of the trip trying to calm him down.

As I unloaded my two bags of groceries into the fridge and cupboard, I swore to myself I wouldn't take him with me again. No desperation for human company would make it worth listening to him and living with that nagging sense that he might be onto something. Why should I try to defend anyone, after what they did to me? Why not just hate them?

The truth was, it was easier to try to defend Trevor to Luke than it would have been to try to defend Joshua or Mackenzie. Trevor didn't really owe me anything, but Joshua and Mack had been my friends. They should know better. They should care. They should have defended me. I felt so horribly alone without them.

Even as those thoughts formed in my mind, I knew the counter to them. Everything I thought about them, they could think about me too. What did it matter that we had been friends for so long, when I had gone ahead and gotten Trevor in trouble? If their actions now could wipe out a past or all other good aspects of the person, didn't my actions towards Trevor also justify them ignoring all my good points?

I hated being able to see both sides of an issue. Confused, contradictory thoughts filled my mind, buzzing like a swarm of insects.

# CHAPTER 6

# March 3rd: Evelyn

A few days later on a grocery trip I ran into Evelyn. Evelyn was a homeschooler, a year older than me. She had moved into town two years before.

None of us in the local school really knew her, but I'd seen her at the library. She had seemed childish and playful. We had been looking at books on opposite sides of a book-shelf. The shelves were metal ones with just bars for backs, no proper backing, and there were big empty areas where books had recently been pruned from the shelves. I had pulled out a book leaving an opening between the two sides, right where she happened to be standing. "Peekaboo" she had said, smiling. I had put the book back, unsure of how to reply to this strange creature. A minute later her head peeked around the end of the bookshelf and she had called again "Peekaboo."

"Who are you?" I had asked.

"Evelyn Muller, homeschooler extraordinaire." She bobbed up and down just slightly, like a half curtsey.

That was as far as our conversation had gone. Back then I had all the friends I needed. I wasn't interested in speaking to some strange goofball in the library. Now, ostracized by my friends, things felt different.

Exactly one month after the trial, we passed on the street and she stopped me.

"You're Jessica Cincinelli, right?" she asked. "You're not in school anymore, are you?"

"Nope. They didn't want me there." I tried to sound smug about it, because the rejection still hurt.

"I heard. Look... I have to go now, but I was wondering if you'd like to hang out sometime?"

I jumped at the chance, scrounging in my coat pockets for a piece of paper, and then scribbled down my number for her. She promised to call, and a few days later we arranged to meet up.

We walked to the playground behind the school. It was evening and the playground was deserted. The monkey bars were cold to touch, but we climbed them anyway. I sat at the top facing the school. Evelyn braced her legs against the bars so she could hang upside down by her knees, her back to the school, her face out towards the soccer fields. Beyond the fields lay the snow-covered ravine and a row of trees.

"I never attended this school," Evelyn said, "but sometimes when I come here in the evenings and sit like this, I imagined this as an enchanted kingdom with the ravine as the magical wall around it. I wasn't sure whether the wall was meant to keep people in or people out."

It seemed a strange childish fantasy to me. Mackenzie or Destiny would never have talked of such things, unless perhaps the kingdom was from a television show with a particularly good-looking actor. I didn't know what to say. I smiled.

"You think I'm silly," she accused, pulling herself up onto the bars so that she was level with me.

"Yes," I answered, "but I'm not sure yet if that's a bad thing." The comment slipped out before I had a chance to consider how rude it must sound. I put my hand up to my mouth too late to block the words.

Evelyn smiled a wide mischievous grin. "Ah, but I am the evil sorcerer come from the darkest corner of the universe. Beware my magic." She had her legs twisted around the monkey bars for balance and used her hands to pretend to cast a spell on me.

Luke and I had played games plenty of times, where we pretended we were *Star Wars* characters fighting with one another with lightning bolts and the force grip. I recognized Evelyn's play as a variation on this, and, strange as it seemed coming from someone closer to my age, I went along with it. I laughed, grabbing the metal to support myself. I wasn't quite as agile on the monkey bars as Evelyn was, but after pretending to duck from her spell I cast one back at her.

"Do you have any brothers or sisters?" I asked as she dropped down from the monkey bars onto the sand.

"Not one," she said.

"You play like you're twelve," I said.

"Oh, I can be sensible if you want. I like to laugh at life, but I don't have to. We could discuss.... well, what is it your school friends would be discussing if you were with them?"

"I don't have school friends." My throat was tight.

"You still miss them," she said, looking down at the footprints in the snow.

"People I played with since I was a baby won't even speak to me anymore." Saying it out loud I could feel the harshness, the unfairness of it. I turned towards the fields and yelled out into the empty space. "Idiots. Jerks and idiots." Then I turned back towards Evelyn and said more quietly "that's what they all are." I had yelled as though trying to reach those houses beyond the ravine. Mackenzie lived in that direction, as did Joshua. I was grateful though that the fields and the trees around the ravine were there and there was little chance that anyone out there could actually hear. I didn't really want them to know how much they'd hurt me.

"Come on," Evelyn said. She dropped down off the monkey bars and started a slow steady jog. I ran after her. We went around the building and then followed the residential street that met the school in a t-intersection. The subdivision had only six blocks to it, and my house was on the second to last block. Evelyn led me past my house, and up to the very end of the street where there was a small forest. Behind it the ground sloped down steeply towards an old abandoned farmyard and then the still snow-covered fields. The farmyard had been unused for quite a while; the fields rented out to the farmer on the other side of the highway.

The old farm sheds were all standing at a sharp slant, as though they were just waiting for the right moment to collapse. We gave them a wide berth as we went into the old barn. The path was packed down. Someone had been coming here throughout the winter.

My eyes needed a minute to adjust to the darkness in the

barn. Along the far wall were some stalls, the boards rotted and falling away, but the floor seemed solid and dry.

The only furniture – if it could be called furniture – was a dark, blue, old-fashioned trunk sitting about a foot from the left wall. As Evelyn opened it I could see why it wasn't pushed back against the wall. The top third lifted up on little hinges, and without the space between it and the wall she would be unable to open it. The whole thing was metal, with one of the back corners rusting and starting to flake away.

Evelyn pulled a woolen blanket from the trunk and spread it out over the floor. "Mom bought the trunk at an estate sale last year. She wanted to use it as a coffee table but it's too rusted out for that, so she gave it to me."

We sat down on the blanket.

"I come here to read," Evelyn said. "My dad knows the owner. There's a well near the sheds that we have to be careful about, but the rest of the place isn't that bad. My dad insists on coming by once a year to check the structural stability. It's really quite safe."

"Your own secret hideout," I said looking around.

Evelyn smiled, happy that I approved of it.

"What do you read?" I asked.

Her smiled widened. "Everything," she said. "Well, not everything. I'm working my way through Elizabeth Gaskell's work right now."

I shrugged and shook my head. "Who is that?"

"A contemporary of Charles Dickens. He helped edit her book *North and South*. It's got a bit of the flavour of *Pride and Prejudice*, but set in the setting of a manufacturing town. The author knew Florence Nightingale's family, and I think that's reflected in the sections about general versus personal concern."

I vaguely remembered watching *North and South* on Netflix, but I was still lost. "General versus personal concern?"

"Yeah. The heroine saves the hero, and the hero thinks it's a sign she loves him. She's horrified because like Florence Nightingale she wanted to believe women can care for and look after people without it being taken as a sign they are in love with the person. She explains she'd do the same thing for anyone, and of course he's crushed. Later though, she realizes that caring for everyone isn't enough to give her life meaning, and that she does love him specifically." Her tone made it sound like she disapproved of the last bit.

"So it is a romance novel?"

"Oh, it's a romance novel alright," she said. Then she shrugged. "People can hide a lot in novels."

She was probably right, but I tried to think of anything serious in the novels I read. I had mainly been reading romance novels, but recently I had read a few of the fantasy novels Chad had left behind when he went to college. The fantasy novels had a bit of a theme about good vs evil, and how the good might move into evil if it wasn't tempered by quite a bit of human liberty. I didn't read all that much though.

"How do you get all that – that stuff - from a romance novel?" I asked.

She was swaying slightly from side to side. Her thick blond hair was hitting against her coat. Her jeans were wet at the bottom, from the snow.

"Partly it is because Mrs. Gaskell is an older writer, and they made themes a bit more explicit then. Partly I think it is practice. Mom did a Masters in English Lit. before she went into nursing, and she's kind of drilled me in that type of analysis ever since I started reading Berenstain Bears."

I laughed. "Ok, now I'm picturing a miniature version of you doing book reports on the literary themes of *Frog and Toad.*"

"Yep, that was my childhood."

I still wasn't sure what to make of Evelyn but for all her strangeness, I liked her. She reminded me a bit of Luke and how it would take only a few second for him to go from making profound statements to seeming like a child half his age. Luke understood things in a different way and it made him seem out of sync at times.

Walking home that night I wondered if Evelyn could be on the spectrum too. I'd read that girls tend to hide autism better than guys, and that's part of why there are more guys diagnosed. I'd even occasionally wondered if I might be autistic, but I'd never been diagnosed, since I hadn't, until recently, had trouble socializing or in school.

Maybe Evelyn was autistic too, either diagnosed or un-diagnosed. I was worried if I asked her, she'd think I was being critical and be offended. Not everyone realized being autistic wasn't a bad thing. There were still kids at school who said, "that's autistic" when what they meant was "that's creepy" or "that's disgusting." I couldn't picture Evelyn using the term that way, but she still might find the question rude. I was being given a second chance to be considered a real person - a second chance at having a friend – and I wasn't about to throw that away.

# CHAPTER 7

# March 6th: The Coffeeshop

Three days later Evelyn called me again, and at her suggestion, we went to the coffee shop downtown.  It was a popular hangout place for teens, with all the fancy coffees not available anywhere else in town. The walls were decorated with paintings local artists hoped to sell, and a collection of carved ducks overflowed from a display case to one side of the counter where we ordered steamed milk.

There wasn't much seating room, only four tables with about a dozen chairs between them. To get to an empty table at the back of the room we had to push past where a group of my old classmates sat. Neither Joshua nor Mackenzie were there, nor Destiny, Trevor or Martin, but Madison was there with three or four others from our class.

Evelyn greeted them, and they shuffled their chairs tighter to allow us move past them. I didn't say a word to them, but pretended they weren't there.

One part of my brain told me I was being petty, treating them with the same silence that they treated me with. Another part of my brain knew it was not *my* being petty, when they were the ones who decided to shun me. I wished either or both sides of my brain would shut up, because I didn't like thinking about the whole thing.

I didn't acknowledge the other teenagers because I didn't want Evelyn to see them not respond. I didn't want her to see the hurt I still felt about being cut out of the lives of people I had known since toddlerhood. They were like strangers now, but strangers I still longed to talk and joke with.

I sat down with my back to them. I wanted to turn around and see what they were doing. I didn't know if I wanted them glaring at me or if I wanted them to be ignoring me. I wasn't sure which would hurt more. I didn't let myself look.

I fixed my eye on a painting of the grain elevators that used to stand guard over the town. I didn't even know what to say to Evelyn now. Why had we come here? Why did we risk coming here? Realizing I had been about to start chewing at my nails again, I tucked my hands under the table.

Evelyn asked me about how I was finding homeschooling. I started explaining about the courses I was taking, and she admitted she wasn't taking any courses herself. Instead she was doing what she called "unschooling." She chose what she wanted to learn and learned it. Her parents insisted she would have to write the standardized tests next year, so she could have a normal high school transcript, but it was up to her how she prepared for them.

"I can't imagine my mom agreeing to that," I said wistfully. She explained that her parents hadn't agreed at first either, but she had shown her parents she could work on her own and eventually they had agreed.

"It's not radical unschooling," she said, "because I do have to do the standardized tests at the end."

"Radical unschooling?" I asked.

She explained that there were lots of unschoolers who didn't believe in doing anything that looked remotely like schoolwork and shunned school subjects themselves in favour of project based learning and practical skill building and such. They didn't worry about getting into university because they didn't believe it necessary for a fulfilling life.

I asked Evelyn why she was homeschooling. Her story wasn't as dramatic as mine. She wasn't bullied or betrayed, but when she had been in school she had this constant nagging sense of not fitting in. She liked to read and not just romance novels or teen books, but nonfiction. Her family talked about politics and literature. Her dad had written books. Both parents were intellectuals, and their love of intellect had set Evelyn apart from her classmates at a young age, so by grade four school felt intolerable. Her dad had given her lessons at the kitchen table when she first started homeschooling, but over the years she took on more and more responsibility for her education herself.

I started wondering whether I could convince Mom to let me unschool too. Maybe if I proved to her that I could take charge of my own education she would let me. The correspondence courses felt a bit like a waste of time. They had way too much review in them.

When I went home I started thinking about what I could study, in addition to my correspondence courses. I didn't really know how to start. Reading Wikipedia wouldn't be enough. I thought about watching documentaries online but that probably wouldn't count either. The local library had a pretty limited non-fiction section. I could order books through interlibrary loan, but I'd have to figure out ahead of time what topics I wanted. What was I interested in?

It occurred to me that I hadn't finished reading *King Lear*. Even though Mr. Mercer seemed to think it was relevant to my whole situation, I had dropped it as soon as I dropped out of school. I had returned the school's loaner copy, but there were copies online I could read. I plunked myself down and powered up my laptop.

There were plenty of copies of *King Lear* online. I had the option of ones with simplified text right next to the Shakespearean, but that felt like cheating. I settled for a page that had the whole script together on one page.

After about a hundred lines of *King Lear* I switched to reading Facebook.

I hadn't touched Facebook since leaving school, and I had unfriended most of my friends before that. My notifications were all updates on relative's posts. With so few friends left, Facebook's algorithms were having trouble finding anything interesting for me. I searched for Mackenzie's profile. I could only see the public posts, but her profile picture had been updated to what I guessed was a picture from her last party. I could see Joshua talking to Destiny in the background.

I looked up Joshua's Facebook profile next. There were a few memes public, nothing else. There was nothing to tell me how he was doing, or if he was missing me. Did he think of me, as I still thought of him? I closed the browser, then reopened it to Facebook again.

What could I post?  I wrote "no night lasts forever." I set the privacy status to public. It was vague and nonsensical in a way, but I had hope. Maybe, just maybe, the lonely night I had been living through was about to fade away.

# CHAPTER 8

# March 10th & 15th: Damian

My optimism seemed justified. The next few days I was too busy to think much about the classmates who would no longer speak to me.

"Where are we going?" I asked. Evelyn had insisted we pack a picnic lunch, coming over to my house and helping slice up cucumbers for fancy sandwiches.

"You realize there's still a foot of snow on the ground?" It wasn't exactly picnic weather.

"Don't worry. I have plans."

She led me the three blocks it takes to get downtown. I went through the possible options for a picnic. I thought the park downtown was a poor choice, since it had only one bench against the sidewalk.

We didn't stop at the park.

"Here we are," she said, pushing the door to Gary's Automotive. The inside was poorly lit and smelly. I had never liked mechanic's shops and I couldn't imagine why we had come to this one. Maybe we were just picking up a car.

The customer area had only one chair and a small coffee table. Evelyn swung open the door labeled "employees only" and called out, "Damian, Damian, where are you?"

A young man with slightly reddish hair and a bit of a goatee came walking over, rubbing his hands on his blue coveralls. His smile was wide and welcoming. "You came," he said, "and I see you brought a friend." He was looking me over. "Jessica, right? Come in the back."

"We brought lunch," Evelyn said.

"Perfect timing. I'm waiting for the next appointment." Damian led us into the shop. There were two lawn chairs there, which Damian motioned for us to take. He sat on the cement.

I knew Damian vaguely from school and had even seen him at the occasional party, but since he had been two grades above me, and a few years below Chad's grade, we hadn't spoken. I was impressed he knew my name. I knew he had been working part time even while in high school. He had probably been working full time since graduating.

"So, you're out of school now," he said.

I wasn't sure if it was a statement or a question. When I didn't answer he continued to speak: "Out of school and hanging around with this lunatic." He was grinning at Evelyn as he said it. She kicked playfully at him, but he responded by leaning his head against her knee.

"Cucumber sandwich?" she offered, pulling them out of her backpack.

I wondered if Damian was still saving up money for

college. College is more expensive for us small town folks, since we can't live with our parents while we attend classes. Or maybe he had just decided to stay here.

Most people left town when they graduated, but a few always stayed. At times the idea of staying had sounded nice. It would mean having one's life rolled out in front of one. You'd have no big changes, no getting lost in the city. Other times I'd felt disdain for those who would stay in town. Why settle for such a place, with so few options for work or entertainment? My classmates behaviour after the trial had just confirmed the idea that those who stayed were fools. Who would risk staying in such a place where one could be hated so easily?

Damian seemed nice though. He seemed friendly. I could picture him staying here. He'd marry someone, get her pregnant, and raise a family. Maybe small-town life suited him.

"Earth to Jessica. Would you like the last sandwich?" Evelyn's voice broke through my idle wonderings.

"Umm... yes. I mean no. Do you want it? I'm fine."

"You can have it, Jessica. It's okay."

"Maybe Damian wants it," I said. Mom had drilled into my head how much boys eat. She was always offering Chad the last of everything, when he was around.

"I've got to get back to work," Damian said, standing up. "Thanks for the lunch though."

I wondered if we had to get up to, but Evelyn stayed seated. We waited, watching, as Damian worked.

Damian had a car, so on his next day off the three of us drove out to one of the small lakes nearby. It was a lake I hadn't been to before. Damian parked the car on the shoulder of the gravel road.

"There's a road right to Miroque," Evelyn said, "but it's snowed in right now."

"Okey-dokey," I answered.

"It's not a road," Damian said. "It's a path."

"It's a road! You've driven on it."

"Yes, I've driven on it, and that is how I know it is a path, not a road."

Evelyn stuck her tongue out at him. He grabbed her backpack from the back seat of the car and swung it over one shoulder before heading off through the snow.

If there was a road, it must have been extremely narrow. The trees were far enough apart to accommodate one vehicle, but passing would be impossible. There were little clearings though where a car could wait while another car passed. The route went up a steep hill and then turned before winding down to the lake.

We came to a clearing about twenty meters wide. It was hard to tell with the snow covering, but it looked like a person might be able to back a vehicle up and unload a boat there during the summer. The only man-made thing visible was a blue tarp half covered in snow.

"There's a fire pit here somewhere, but we probably don't need to worry about finding it with all this snow." Evelyn said. "Grab some wood from under the tarp."

Damian and I went for the wood. We brushed some of the snow off the top with our coat-sleeves before pulling the tarp back. There was snow under the tarp too, but we selected what looked like the driest logs and brought them over to where Evelyn had trampled down a small circle. She laid a platform of logs on the snow and then built a little pyramid on top of that. Evelyn had paper, matches and snack supplies in her backpack.

Evelyn coaxed the fire up to a roaring blaze and then let it slowly fade to embers, so we could roast marshmallows and make s'mores. It seemed oddly quiet. I was used to the larger crowds that would gather at bush parties, where alcohol made everyone noisier. I could hear the birds in the background.

"These s'mores are better," I said as I licked the chocolate and marshmallow off my fingers, "than marshmallow vodka shots."

"Marshmallow vodka shots?" Evelyn asked, her eyebrows raised.

"If the outsides of the marshmallow are melted right but the inside is a bit too hard still you can pull the tops off the sticks and use them for a shot glass. I should tell you the story of where I first heard of that. Destiny and I were out with a couple of twelfth graders last year. We had a fire going by the river and a police officer pulled up. We thought he might tell us off for underage drinking, but instead he showed us how to make shot-glasses."

Damian laughed. "You know," he said after a minute or two pause, "it really is amazing anyone cared about Trevor's stunt with the snowmobile, when you consider everything else people get away with here."

"It was Mr. Henderson who pushed it. He knew it would be one of the McNickels and he asked around until he found out Trevor had come walking into town with the three of us.

He insisted we be interrogated. No one would have cared or done a thing if he hadn't pushed the point."

"I wonder if he's content with the sentencing."

"It's the scholarship that's the real punishment," I said. "Trevor was counting on a full scholarship."

"Maybe he'll have to work and save like the rest of us mortals."

I snorted. "Those are probably not his strong suits."

"University is just one year away for me," Evelyn said. "This time next year I'll have sent applications all over Canada."

"Two years for me," I said. "Two more years of home-schooling, I guess."

I wasn't quite sure, but I thought Damian grimaced. Then he grabbed another log for the fire, pushing at the half-burnt logs and sending up a fury of sparks. When he was done he snuggled close to Evelyn and pulled her against him. I watched as they rested against each other.

No one said anything else for a bit and then I hesitantly began to sing a simple song.

I paused, but Evelyn invited me to sing more. So, I did and then when I finished my song Damian announced it was his turn to sing. I was surprised.

He shifted Evelyn so she wasn't resting on him anymore and leaned in towards the fire slightly. He took a deep breath before beginning. His was a rolling happy song about bankrupt farmers turning pirates.

"Where did you learn that song?" I asked. It was a song played on the oldies station.

"It's what we listen to at the shop when Gary's there."

"What do you listen to when he's not there?"

"When he's not there I'm working twice as hard and not listening to anything really." he said.

"You've practiced the song. That's not your first time singing it."

He shrugged. "My sisters like it when I sing it to them."

We sat, silently for a moment. Then I turned to Evelyn. "Your turn to sing," I said, but she didn't sing. She just went to put wood on the fire.

"Make a wish," she commanded, as she sat back down, bringing a small container from her purse with her. She opened it. "Flour," she explained. "Make a wish, and throw some into the fire." One by one we made our wishes silently, and watched as the fire flared up to devour the flour. I wished I could go back in time, erase the past half year and not have been there when Trevor sunk the snowmobile. It was a foolish wish I knew could not come true.

When the fire was over, Evelyn mixed a bit of the ashes into her container of flour. "For next time," she said.

The hike back to the car was cold, but as we left the forest and stepped onto the road we could see the northern lights dancing in the sky, a ribbon of pale green.

# CHAPTER 9

# March 16th: Family

"I'm worried about you," Mom said the next day, sitting down across from me at the kitchen table for our once-a-week check up on how my schoolwork was progressing.

"You don't need to worry," I said. "I'll get all the courses done in time. I promise."

"Not the schoolwork," she said, "the social life. I'm glad you've got some new friends now, but you used to have more friends."

"I'm okay, mom. I think I'm going to get along with Evelyn and Damian. I think we're going to be friends. I have you and dad and Luke. I have more time to read and help around the house. In a few years, I'll be away at college anyway."

"Maybe you could go back to school next year. Trevor will have graduated and be gone. You had good friends before. Give them time and they will come around."

"Okay, and if they do come around? Then what? How can I ever trust them again? How can I be friends with people who will treat me this way just because I say or do something they disagree with? Besides, I've enjoyed being home. I like the quiet."

"Maybe you should go stay in Edmonton. Maybe you could stay with Chad or my sister and go to school there."

"I'm fine mom. Really, I am. Besides, I want to unschool next year. I already told you that."

"Ummm," she said noncommittally.

"You will consider it, right mom?"

"I don't know. I want to know you're going to graduate, and what would you do with all your time anyway?"

"I would set my own goals and study what I want. I'm sure I could."

"We'll see. Let's look at what schoolwork you did this week."

Mom didn't mark my work. That was done by the correspondence teachers. What she wanted to check was that I was getting some work done, so I had my day timer spread out in front of me open to the week. I had divided up each subject into as many parts as I had weeks left, and then divided each week's goals into daily goals. I always scheduled the largest chunk of my schoolwork for Mondays, letting the amount of work gradually peter out as it got further in the week. I was only a month in, but I knew my own work habits.

I would work extra hard on Monday and get some of Tuesday's work done. Then on Tuesday I would try to do half of Wednesday's work as well, and so on, each day increasing the amount I was ahead so that by Thursday night I had everything done for the week.

I liked the little black streaks across my to-do list. After everything for the day was streaked out, I could go for a walk or read a book or do other things. I wasn't allowed to watch television, not even streaming shows on my computer. That was one rule my parents did set fearing that I would just binge watch television all day. They need not have worried. There weren't that many good shows anyway, and it wasn't my style.

When I was done my work, I'd text Evelyn. When it felt warm we'd go hike through the snow or sit in the shelter of the barn, but since the weather was frequently uncooperative we'd end up staying indoors. She would come to my house, or I'd head over to her place. Damian joined us when he could, and sometimes we watched him work at the automotive shop.

I was walking home from the automotive shop when I ran into Trevor. The moment I saw him on the sidewalk, coming towards me, my eyes went to the houses nearby. Where could I run, if I needed help? Years of trick-or-treating in the neighbourhood had taught me that the senior citizens were slow to get to the doors and couldn't be depended upon in an emergency. It was only four-thirty in the afternoon, so most adults would probably be at work. There was a car in the dentist's driveway though. Perhaps his wife was home. I decided that would be the place I'd run to if I needed help.

My hand reached into my pockets. I'd read online that car keys could be used as a weapon, but I didn't have any with me, only some scraps of paper and a pencil stub. My fingers wrapped around the pencil stub.

The closer he got to me the more my heart pounded. I forced myself to stare straight ahead and past him. We were just a step or two past one another when I heard him hiss at me. "Bitch."

I kept walking, pretending I couldn't hear. It was good I didn't still have the pepper spray in my pocket. I might have been tempted to use it. I wondered how I was supposed to know when to use it anyway. Exactly how scary would he have to be to justify my using it?

# CHAPTER 10

# March 20th: Church

The next Sunday, Evelyn came to church with my family and me. It was her idea. She'd never been to church and was curious. I fidgeted in my jeans and t-shirt and she sat beside me in a worn purple dress. Her eyes were glued to the large wooden cross in the front. My mind wandered.

Each step of the service was familiar to me, the liturgy having changed only slightly with each minister that came and went after his or her three-year placement. The call to worship blended together in my mind with every other call to worship. I read the bolded print in the pamphlet without thinking about the words. In unison, we all recited a prayer of confession and listened to the minister's assurance that we were forgiven. I wondered briefly what that meant in a place where people I once considered friends no longer spoke to me.

I didn't hear much of the sermon. Instead I stared out the window at the clear blue sky. A few birds flew past and I imagined what it would be like to fly with them. The closing hymn jolted me out of my daydreams.

When the service ended we all shook hands with those near us and greeted one another. I hated this part. I'd always stand there awkwardly. My hand would start to sweat, and I'd rub it roughly against my jeans before shoving it into the hands of some friendly old lady who would ask how I'm doing in school. Then I'd breathe a sigh of relief when Mom finally herded us to the door to leave.

Evelyn smiled, chatted cheerfully and behaved charmingly, as Dad would later say. Then she looked over at me where I stood and quickly traced the shape of a barn in the air with one hand. I called quickly to Mom that Evelyn and I would walk home.

The church was on the edge of town, next to a field and we skirted around the outside of town to our spot. "Top of the world," Evelyn cried from the hill overlooking our barn. She flung her hands into the air and raced down. I went slower, stumbling over a gopher hole.

"So?" she asked when we were finally sitting on the grass next to the barn. "What do you think?"

"Think about what?"

"What do you think about church?"

"I don't know. It's church. It's okay, I guess."

"Do you believe it?" she asked.

"I guess. I assume there's a God and that Jesus was his son. I don't know. My parents don't make me go anymore, but I feel bad when I don't go."

I picked at a few clover flowers and began to braid their stems together. "What do you believe?" I asked.

She lay back on the grass and closed her eyes for a second or two. Then she opened them, and smiled. "This is heaven," she said. "Lying here, on the grass beside you, staring up into the beautiful blue sky. Watching the birds, feeling the grass dance, and knowing the world is alive. In church, they can talk about heaven coming when we die, but to me heaven is here, now."

"And God?" I asked.

"This is God. The trees are God. The air, and the birds, and the land are all God."

"That sounds a bit like something some of the First Nations believe." We lived on what used to be Cree land and we read bits about Native culture in school, but I didn't know much. Maybe I was wrong.

"Perhaps some, I don't know." We were both silent for a few minutes. Then Evelyn spoke again. "I've always been curious about Native spiritually, but I can't just go out to the reserve and ask them to teach me, can I?"

"I guess not," I said.

"I turn to bits of pre-Christian European and Middle Eastern mythology and instead," she said defiantly. "I believe that God is all powerful, and if that is so then nothing can be outside of God. We are part of God. Thou art a Goddess, Jessica."

"Goddess? Is God a woman?" I was used to the term God and the idea that God was male. I didn't believe that males were better than females, but that God happened to be male just like I happened to be female.

"The divine is beyond all gender," she said, "and yet why shouldn't we sense the divine's presence as the spirit of a woman? Why wouldn't the divine come to us as we are and not just as men are?"

I lay down on the grass too. The sky overhead was beautiful. There were just a few light wispy clouds streaked across the sky, like smears of finger paint or cotton candy.

"Do you pray?" I asked. If the divine was everywhere, in everything, how would one talk to it?

"That depends what you count as prayer. Over the last two years, I've been learning about Wicca. That's what modern witchcraft is called."

"Witchcraft?" My mind filled with images of cauldrons, snakes, frogs and broomsticks.

"It's nothing too weird." She sat up and watched me, measuring my reaction as she spoke. "I do rituals and magic. I light candles and say what could probably be considered prayers. I try to connect with the gods and goddesses people worshiped long ago. I do magic."

I was intrigued. "Magic? What magic?"

"It isn't magic tricks or anything. I don't know how to explain it. It's more...setting one's intention into the world."

"Does it work?"

She lay back down on the grass. "I think it does."

"What about love spells?" I asked. "Can you do love spells?"

"Maybe." I could hear the laughter in her voice. "But would you want a guy caught by a love spell? Wouldn't you want someone who fell in love with you because of who you are?"

I didn't like the truth in what she said, so I argued back.

"Perhaps there's someone so special that the benefits of who he is outweighs how he was caught."

"Do you know such a person?"

"No," I admitted. The only guy I'd really thought about was Joshua and he wasn't all that great. I missed him more than I wanted to admit, even to myself, but he wasn't all that special. "I don't have anyone particular in mind. I'm just curious."

"I've never tried," she said. "But you were thinking of someone just now. I know you were. Spit it out. Who was it?"

"Joshua," I said. "Joshua Chelmers. He and I used to be friends and then we started being more, but he stopped talking to me when everyone else did."

"You miss him, but he's not special enough to try using magic to bring back?"

"Right. Because he's a jerk. He's a stupid, cowardly jerk."

"Glad we've got that straight."

# CHAPTER 11

# March 20th and 21st: Wicca

That evening I googled "Wicca." Wicca has no centralized authority but a principle of "harm none." Some websites tried to sell jewelry, herbs and essential oils. Others had rituals, some more elaborate than others. There were hundreds of different types of pages, some talking about subgroups of wiccans, such as Earth magic or Faery Wicca. I chose one of the websites that wasn't trying to sell me things or deal with a specific subgroup and I texted the link to Evelyn.

"Is this what you mean by Wicca?" I wrote.

The website didn't seem that weird. It mainly talked about trying to live in harmony with nature – whatever that meant – and doing rituals. It also said you find your deity from over two hundred gods or goddesses. You didn't just get to pick and choose, but you have to be open while a deity presents itself. I wondered if I tried what type of deity would present itself to me.

"Close but not quite." She texted a link back.

I had only read the first paragraph when Evelyn texted me again. "Scared yet?"

"Why would I be?" I replied.

"Wicca =/= normal. Am I going to hell?"

The United Church didn't talk much about hell. Our current minister said hell was a state of mind, the suffering one endures when one feels separated from God. The minister before last said a loving God wouldn't condemn anyone to suffering and hell was a later church doctrine that Jesus never taught. Besides that, mom said all religions were a path to God. Evelyn's religion sounded different, but I didn't think Evelyn had anything to fear.

I hated texting. I dialed her number.

"What's up?" she asked.

"I didn't want you to think I was judging you," I said.

"Thanks," she said. "I thought the Goddess was drawing me towards you, but I was still scared of what you'd think when you found out I'm a witch."

"I think I've got to find you a big metal cauldron somehow," I said, trying to lighten the mood.

I hadn't prayed much, outside of church, but that night I did. I wanted to feel the sense of the divine that Evelyn had described. I sat cross legged on my bed. "God," I prayed. "Or Goddess," I added with a little laugh. It seemed weird, but in my mind I imagined a beautiful spirit shining in light, with the light flowing down onto me. I paused unsure of what to say. "Let me feel your presence. Hold me in your light."

At church I'd had moments where I felt God's presence with me, but it was rare. Church was about the minister and the minister's actions as he broke the bread and poured the grape juice we used for communion instead of wine. Church was about listening to lectures on how to be a better person when I was already trying my hardest. Maybe Evelyn was onto something.

The next morning my schoolwork felt particularly dull. I watched a fifteen-minute video about globalization and read the accompanying text for social studies. I sped through math, French, and science. I checked off one topic after another from my to-do list until I could text Evelyn that I was free to go meet her. I broke my family rules and invited myself over to her house instead of waiting to see where she wanted to meet up.

There were no couches in Evelyn's living room, just an assortment of different chairs. I had chosen a wooden rocking chair, while Evelyn sat in a stiff wing-back chair, her legs folded up underneath her. There were four bookshelves in the room, each with plants interspersed among the books. A baby spider plant dangled from a larger spider plant on the bookshelf next to me.

"Teach me about Wicca," I said as soon as we were comfortable in the living room.

"Why?" she asked. "I mean, I wanted you to know I was into it, because it felt weird you not knowing but I was scared of how you might react. I wasn't trying to get you to join me or anything."

"Teach me."

"I don't know how."

"Ok," I said, resigned.

Evelyn bit her lip. "I'll try."

She took me up to her bedroom. She had a desk covered in papers. There was a cage on her dresser with a tiny rodent. "My familiar," she said with a laugh.

My jaw dropped, and I stared at her, startled. I had convinced myself the night before that witchcraft wasn't evil, but I wasn't keen on the idea of rodents being used in spells or attempts at magical possession or anything.

"I'm joking," she said. "She's just a dwarf hamster. I named her Tess, after Tess d'Urberville." I didn't know the reference.

"She's cute," I said. Evelyn took her out and let me hold her for a minute. Her fur was patched white and grey. Her tiny paws had beautiful long toenails. I let her sniff me, watching her claws and her wiggling whiskers. Then I held her up to my face so I could feel her fur against my cheek. When I put her back in the cage she climbed the bars and tumbled back down into a pile of bedding.

I looked around the rest of the room. Evelyn's bed had an old metal frame and a bedspread with little yellow flowers on it. Matching yellow curtains covered Venetian blinds. In front of her window was a wooden filing cabinet.

Evelyn gestured to the filing cabinet. "My altar," she said. An imitation silk-scarf was being used as a tablecloth. There was a small dark red glass pyramid with a little door handle she could open, so she could place things inside. Two candles stood on either side of it. In front was a small bowl.

"When I'm inside I use this for spells or what you could call prayer. I try to do everything outside though, and then I just take what I need."

"What's in the pyramid?" I asked.

"Herbs," she said. She picked it up and opened it, tilting it in her hand so the dried plants fell out. I could recognize the smell of rosemary, but not the others. She crumbled them up and sprinkled them into the little bowl.

"Prayers with props," I said smiling.

"Perhaps that's one way of looking at it," Evelyn said.

# CHAPTER 12

# March 31: Wicca on my Own

Bit by bit over the next few weeks I learned about Evelyn's beliefs and bit by bit I began to share them, adapting similar practices for myself. I didn't dare set up an altar in my room, but I cleared space in my dresser where I could hide some candles. I found a small metal ashtray at a second-hand store, and I scoured it with salt so that I could use it to burn little bits of paper on. I wanted to be able to write out my prayers and then burn them. I bought essential oils to help cover the smell of the candles and burnt paper.

My prayers were simple. I prayed for strength. I prayed the nightmares I was having about my classmates mocking me would go away. I prayed that I would know it was okay to pray that way.

I let myself imagine beings of light and love weaving through the fabric of our lives. I imagined spirits guiding me, holding me, encouraging me. I let myself sense God's presence in my life.

I was divided within myself. One part of me knew that I was just imagining things. The trees were just trees, the ground just soil. The guiding spirits were just my own imagination. Another part believed that I could be tapping into something greater than myself. Was this not just another way of praying? Connecting to the spirit of all things?

On the day of the new moon my parents drove Luke into Edmonton for a doctor's appointment, and they stayed to have supper with Chad. I knew they wouldn't return till late and so I took my candles, my little metal tray, some paper, a pencil, matches and a glass of water outside with me. It took three trips before I had everything ready. I sat down on the grass. I leaned back against the one beautiful shade tree we had in our yard.

"Sister tree," I whispered to the tree, my fingers reaching behind me to press into the cracks of its rough bark. I imagined my spirit and the tree's touching, like two lights coming together for a brief moment. I imagined roots growing down from me into the ground.

I imagined light and love spreading through both the tree and me. I imagined it spreading through the ground and out into the town, pictured it surrounding everyone. A lump caught in my throat. I thought of Joshua and Mackenzie. I wondered what they were doing right then. Did they ever think of me? Did they ever miss me as I missed them?

I missed Joshua's arms around me and his awkward smile. I missed joking with him. I missed Mackenzie's storytelling, and the energy that Destiny brought to things. I missed

Madison with her constant worrying about everything. How could they be so completely unwilling to talk to me? Didn't they know I had no options? I couldn't lie. I'd never been good at lying. Didn't they know that?

I stared down at my candles, my pencil and paper, and the little tray: the silly tools of my attempts at magic.

I drew a deep breath and let it go, slowly.

Could I do magic? Could I somehow reach out and connect with these friends? Could I draw them back to me with magic? Hope flew through me.

I took another deep breath and let it go, slowly.

I didn't want to give them the opportunity to reject me again. I didn't trust myself. I didn't trust any magic I could do, any prayer or spell, to really bring them back to me.

I would not try to draw them to me. I would let them go. I took the sheet of paper and I began to write every hurtful thing they had ever said or done to me. I wrote about every feeling of rejection. Then I ripped the paper into quarters, and carefully burned each piece. As the paper burned I whispered over and over: *I forgive you, and I am free of you. All that is over and I forgive you for it. I am free of you.*

Then I dipped my fingers into the glass of water, and touched my head. I couldn't feel the water through my hair, so I poured from the glass directly onto my head. I took a bit of water, and drew the peace symbol on my forehead. Not very imaginative, but that was all I could think of. Goddess, bless me, I prayed. Wash away all anger. Make me clean.

By the time my parents came home I'd hid everything and was sitting at the computer reading. After ordering a book on

Wicca online, I forced myself to do some reading for my social studies course.

"Jessica," Mom said, smiling when she came in. "How was your evening?"

"It was really good Mom. I did some of the work I was planning on doing tomorrow. I'll be able to meet up with Evelyn earlier."

Mom pursed her lips ever so slightly and then took on a wide, forced smile. "Could you be home in time to help me with supper? It's been so long since we've had company. I've invited the Chelmers over tomorrow night."

The Chelmers meant Joshua and his parents. Joshua's older brother – Chad's friend – was away at university. Mom still seemed to think she could bring my old friends and me back together.

"No, mom," I said. "Please don't."

"It's already done, sweetie," her smile was smaller, slightly worried.

"You can't have! You know Joshua hasn't spoken to me since... since he decided to be a jerk. You can't expect me to sit there politely at the table with him pretending we're all great friends. You can't."

"I've already invited them," she said firmly. "Now I need to go say goodnight to your brother."

# CHAPTER 13

# April 1th: The Shop

It was raining out the next day, so Evelyn and I arranged to meet at Gary's Automotive. We arrived at the same time.

"Does Gary mind us being here?" I asked as we entered the building.

"Mind what?" Gary said, looking up from where he was standing with Damian, staring at the engine of a station-wagon.

"You don't mind us sitting here, watching Damian work, do you Mr. Aymers?" Evelyn had a bright smile.

"This isn't a coffee shop," he said gruffly, "or a high school. Don't you have some place better to be?"

"But it's raining out," Evelyn said. "And we won't disturb Damian. You always get your work done, don't you, Damian?"

"Sure, I do," Damian affirmed.

"Just stay out of the way. Insurance won't cover if you get

yourself squashed under a vehicle." Gary had a soft spot for Evelyn. He motioned with his hand towards the lawn chairs.

We sat down. Evelyn pulled a sketchpad and some pencils out of her backpack and started to draw.

"My mom's invited Joshua's whole family over for supper tonight," I said. "Can you believe it?"

Her eyebrows shot up. "That's going to be interesting. You two haven't even talked since the incident, have you?" Her hands didn't leave the paper.

"Nope. I didn't even get the dignity of a breakup text."

"Well, that's definitely going to be an interesting dinner. That's tonight you said, right?"

I nodded. Tonight was a bit black hole waiting to pull me in. I couldn't see past it.

Normally when I worried I could try to picture the situation ahead of time and imagine different possibilities, but the possibilities for supper were too painful. Joshua not speaking to me at supper would be so much worse than him not speaking to me at school, but then perhaps he would come and pretend nothing had happened between us and we were still friends. Would I be able to stay calm enough to deal with that? Would it just hurt too much to go back to him not speaking afterwards? Or perhaps he wouldn't come at all. I didn't let myself dwell on that. I couldn't plan. I couldn't picture how things would work to reassure myself. There was no real way for things to work. There was no way that would not hurt.

Evelyn had been speaking, but I had missed hearing what she said. I shook myself out of my worries.

"Let's plan on something different tomorrow night. How about you come over for dinner at my place?"

I nodded.

"You too, Damian," she added, raising her voice to catch his attention.

"What's that?" he called, looking up from the motor. His hands were covered in grease.

"You're coming for dinner at my place tomorrow."

"I get to meet your parents at last?" He was happy.

"You've met them! You've met them lots of times."

"I've said hello to them when picking you up. That doesn't exactly constitute meeting them."

"I don't know" Gary said, not looking up from the motor, "this sounds pretty serious to me."

"Jessica's coming too," Evelyn said blushing. "This isn't a big thing."

"Whatever you say, dear," Gary kept his face straight, but his voice laughed.

Damian stepped in. "Oooh... watch out. Even I don't dare to call her dear."

"Will you two cut it out already?" Evelyn was blushing badly now.

"Forget tomorrow night. How am I going to manage to-night?" Dinner tomorrow with Evelyn and Damian would be a walk in the park. Dinner with Joshua was terrifying. No one had much to offer though.

"There's a newspaper over there that might distract you," Damian said, gesturing a cluttered counter. "Check out page three."

I grabbed the paper and flipped to the page he mentioned. There was an article about an anti-bullying day at the school.

The accompanying picture showed Destiny, Madison and a few other girls in bright pink t-shirts.

"Barf," I said. There were no suitable words for my disgust.

Evelyn looked at the article over my shoulder. "What is it?"

"It is an anti-bullying campaign in the school, and here's two of the most clueless, least self-aware people ever as the face of it."

"I've heard of the whole wear-pink to school thing but never quite understood the point of it."

"There isn't one," I said, shaking my head in disgust. "It's just a way for the popular kids to tell themselves how great they are."

I sighed. I knew that wasn't fair of me. I took another deep breath and explained the other side. "It started out good," I said. "It started out with people wearing pink in support of a boy who had been bullied for wearing pink, but now..."

"Now it's just a marketing gimmick," Damian interrupted. "They sell special pink t-shirts for it. Kids might as well just buy a plain one and then you can use it on breast cancer awareness days too."

Evelyn was still reading the article and looking at the picture. "The girls at the front here are ones you've mentioned, right?"

"Destiny and Madison."

"There's a quote here from one of them." She read the quote out to us. "*Destiny Sprat says the anti-bullying campaign is important to her because 'we want everyone to be friends here. That's what's great about living in a small town.'*"

"Barf and double barf. They couldn't have found anyone else to interview instead?"

Evelyn tossed the paper back onto the counter.

"There are all too many campaigns in school these days," Gary grumbled. "We didn't have any of that when I was a kid."

"Was paper invented back when you were a kid?" Evelyn teased.

I laughed, but my stomach was still clenched up in nervousness about the Chelmers coming for supper.

# CHAPTER 14

# April 1th again: Chelmers

I dressed carefully, choosing a fluffy pink sweater and my best fitting pair of jeans. I even tried to fix my hair up a bit. Luke watched from the hallway. "Ooooh, your boyfriend's coming," he called. I slammed the door. Joshua wasn't my boyfriend. At least not anymore.

Joshua didn't come for supper. A mixture of relief and disappointment washed over me as I watched Mom welcome Mr. and Mrs. Chelmers into the house. Mrs. Chelmers carried a large bowl of salad, which Mom took from her and set on the kitchen table.

"I'm sorry, when I talked to you on the phone I didn't know Joshua had other commitments," Mrs. Chelmers told my mom. She looked at me with an expression of sympathy. "And of course, Matt is away at university still. He mentions Chad sometimes, though not so much lately. How is Chad doing with his courses?"

We'd had the Chelmers over for dinner about twice a year for as long as I remember. They are old family friends. Normally Joshua not being able to come too would be a reason to switch the date, but this time it was obviously just a polite excuse for his not wanting to come.

Joshua's absence meant I could politely disappear till dinner was served. I sat for a few minutes in my bedroom, rocking back and forth. I had feared his arrival, but as soon I knew he wasn't coming, I felt the pain of his absence again. Even if it was going to have been an awkward, awful meal, at least I'd have had the chance to see him. I'd have a hope that things could somehow have been fixed between him and I, over Mom's pork chops and applesauce. But I guess he didn't even want to try.

It was kind of silly how we started being more than friends. We were at a bush party together, drinking and laughing with about twenty others around a big bon fire. I'd had a second beer, which I almost never did, so I was in a little less control of myself than normal. A drunk out-of-towner was trying to hit on me, and I was trying to push the guy away without pushing him towards the bonfire, and Joshua had come up beside me and wrapped his arm around me. "Get lost," he said to the out-of-towner. "Stop picking on my girl." Then he kissed me. When the drunk moved on I had pushed him back a bit saying he could stop pretending, but he whispered, "I wasn't meaning to pretend." I kissed my tall, lanky, childhood friend back.

Getting physically intimate – whether just kissing or more – at a bush party wasn't exactly an auspicious start to a relationship. In fact, according to the customs of the youth of our town it wasn't the start to anything. I know some of my friends did things I wouldn't, knowing that it means nothing to the guy the next day. So, I'd been pleased when Joshua had kissed me at school the next day and we had walked to classes hand in hand, our fingers intertwined. We had been involved for about a year after that.

I didn't want to cry. I didn't want to look like I had been crying. I washed my face in the washroom again and returned to my bedroom to wait.

My cat, Sandy, came and nuzzled her head against my arm, looking for attention. When I started petting her back she rolled over so I could scratch her belly. "Are you going to be my familiar?" I whispered, rubbing my face against her fur.

When it was time to sit down for dinner, I positioned my-self across from Luke. Normally I avoid watching him while he eats – he still forgets to close his mouth – but this time I wanted to be facing someone I could watch without thinking about Josh.

Dad and Mr. Chelmers compared the last winter's ice fish-ing successes. Dad gracefully agreed that Mr. Chelmers had caught the larger fish. Mom had a whole litany of questions for Mrs. Chelmers. Did she have any special plans for the summer or for her garden. How was Matt enjoying univer-sity? How was Joshua enjoying school?

"Is Joshua dating someone new?" Luke asked. I had been trying to coax him to find that out for me through kids at school, but I hadn't meant for him to ask Joshua's parents right in front of me!

All eyes turned to me. I forced myself to look at Mrs. Chelmers, to wait for her answer with a facade of indifference.

"Well, I don't know," she seemed flustered for a moment. "He doesn't really tell me these things, you know. He's mentioned Mackenzie a couple of times. There was something about a party."

It was alright then. It would have been Mackenzie's party, that Mrs. Chelmers had heard about. Mackenzie was never interested in Joshua. They were just good friends.

"How are you enjoying the correspondence courses?" Mr. Chelmers asked.

"I'm actually enjoying it quite a bit," I paused. I didn't know how to answer the question. I had two options. The ending I wanted to give that sentence was to say that the courses were so much more enjoyable than sitting in class when everyone in class hated me. However, I didn't know if I could say that without sounding hostile, and I didn't want to sound hostile. So, I went for my second option. "I'm finding that I read quicker than most teachers lecture."

"I can imagine so," Mr. Chelmers laughed.

"How about a round of bridge after supper?" Mom asked. I was grateful. Only the adults would be needed to play bridge. I could escape upstairs. I sent a text to Evelyn telling her that Joshua hadn't come and an email to Damian asking him to drive me to Evelyn's house tomorrow if it was raining still.

# CHAPTER 15

# April 2th: Mullers

It rained. When Damian and I arrived at Evelyn's house, she was sitting by the front window, watching the water trail across the window pane, but Mrs. Muller was still bustling around the kitchen.

"Mother's always in a panic over serving dinner to anyone," Evelyn explained. "Grandmother was the absolute perfect host, and none of her children feel they can live up to her legacy."

Mrs. Muller smiled but didn't answer.

"You're doing fine, dear. Relax." Mr. Muller came in from the library and kissed his wife quickly. "I'm sure Eve's friends are unlikely to burn the house down on account of too much or little salt in the sauces."

Damian answered, grinning. "Oh no, Mr. Muller. That offense would only just warrant kidnapping your daughter. I think you'd have to do something like burn the meat entirely to convince us to light any fires."

"See? Nothing to worry about at all, dear." With that we all went into the dining room.

It was like traveling into the past and entering a monastery. The dining room tabletop must have been at least three inches thick, solid wood. It looked too heavy to move. How they had ever gotten it into the room? Perhaps they built it here. The chairs were made of the same dark wood with tall straight backs on them. There were candle holders mounted on the walls around the room. The candles weren't lit. Mr. and Mrs. Muller took the end seats, with Mrs. Muller closest to the kitchen. Evelyn and I sat together on one side; Damian sat opposite us.

Evelyn explained that the food was a beef korma on rice with naan bread. I learned that korma was a spicy East-Indian stew. The recipe called for lamb, but the local grocery stores didn't carry it.

Evelyn's parents directed their questions first towards Damian.

"So, at nineteen, why are you hanging around my seventeen-year-old daughter?" Mr. Muller asked.

"Dad," Evelyn protested. Mr. Muller was as bad as Luke for awkward questions!

Mrs. Muller put her hand on Evelyn's arm to calm the protest.

Mr. Muller tore up a piece of naan and dipped it in the korma. He looked at Damian expectantly.

"Well, I... umm.... I promise I've been nothing but a gentleman?" He and Evelyn were both blushing.

"Of course you are," Evelyn said. She was calmer now, almost haughty. "You're a gentleman, and we are *not* dating."

Damian looked down at his plate.

"Evelyn tells us you read quite a bit," Mrs. Muller said, coming to the rescue. "But she hasn't told us what you read. What do you read?"

"Oh, a bit here and there."

"Don't be modest," Evelyn commanded. "He reads all sorts of things. He was explaining the other day about the use of laser interferometers for measuring gravitational waves."

"That's right up your alley." Mr. Muller grinned at his wife. "You've read about those."

"Well, yes, but I haven't been keeping up on it. Last I heard there was the main LIGOs were shut down for repairs, and the scientists were lamenting the lack of funds for a third LIGO so that they could properly triangulate the direction the waves were coming from."

"Oh, there are some foreign LIGOs opening, and they should be able to coordinate with them for the triangulation...."

I listened, humbled by the knowledge others shared. Luke should have been here, not me. He liked learning about gravity and planets and such. I gathered LIGOs were the observatories that detected gravitational waves, but I couldn't follow much else. Watching Damian talk with Mrs. Muller about them, I wondered why he was still in town. He should be in university, not working at a mechanic's shop.

When the conversation paused Mr. Muller turned to me.

"What about you? What are you reading these days?"

"*King Lear*," I said. I had finished reading the play a day or two before, but I didn't know what else to name. Besides, I had ordered two books about Lear through interlibrary loan, so I would be reading more about the topic soon.

"The weight of this sad time we must obey; Speak what we feel, not what we ought to say," quoted Mr. Muller. Evelyn had not been exaggerating when she had told me her family was academic. I wondered if there was any topic I could have brought up which none of them would have anything to say on.

"Evelyn said you were interested in Wicca too," Mrs. Muller said.

"Yes, I am," I said, at the same time Evelyn said "Mom, hush."

"Oh, right, not in front of Damian," Mrs. Muller continued.

Damian looked up from his food. "I know she is into Wicca. I might not approve, but I know. No need to hide it on my account."

Now it was Evelyn's turn to be embarrassed. "I don't mean to hide it, I just...."

Mr. Muller interrupted. "Perhaps we can focus on *King Lear*, for another moment." I was back on the hot seat, required to give my opinion on a play of which I had only cursory knowledge.

# CHAPTER 16

# April 15th: King Lear

The interlibrary loan books for my *King Lear* study arrived. The first one was fascinating. It was only slightly harder reading than a novel and drew me into the world of London in 1606. I read about the plague that delayed King James' coronation and how the Guy Fawkes Plot had raised the specter of the king's death. The topic of union between England and Scotland under their new Scottish king might have been reflected in King Lear's unwise decision to split his kingdom. Since my goal was to assure Mom I was capable of independent study, I took copious notes.

The second book was harder. I stumbled through the first two chapters before throwing it down in disgust.

I took my problem to Evelyn and Damian, as we shared a picnic lunch behind the automotive shop, next to the garbage bins. We had moved the lawn chairs outside, and Gary had picked up a third chair at a garage sale. We were glad for that, because the grass was pretty sparse, and Gary's cigarette buds littered the area, so we didn't want anyone to have to sit on the ground. It was private though, and Damian could listen for customers.

"The books disagree, and I don't know which one to believe," I said.

Damian laughed. "Ah, the life of an academic."

"It's not a laughing matter," I said. "How am I supposed to do it?"

Evelyn was rummaging in her backpack for a spoon for her yogurt. "Evaluate the different arguments, compare how they come to their different conclusions and then be prepared to argue for whichever one you think is most believable. Ah, here it is." She ripped the lid off the yogurt and dug in.

"I don't know how to do any of that," I said.

"Sure, you do."

"It doesn't come naturally to me, like it does to you."

"You can do it."

"Repeating that doesn't make it true."

"Ok, I won't say it again. But you need to keep having fun with *King Lear* too. You've read it, now you're reading about it. Have you tried acting any of it?"

Of course, I hadn't.

"Let's try," Evelyn said. Her eyes sparkled with excitement. "Out by the old barn tonight, let's try a few scenes."

I just stared at her. Me act? In front of her and Damian?

"It will be fun," she said.

It was Damian who agreed first; was there anything he wouldn't do for her? "I'll be there."

Evelyn beamed at him and offered him the last spoonful of

her yogurt. He let her feed it to him. Then they both turned and stared at me.

I conceded. "I guess I'll be there too."

"We'll need scripts," Evelyn said. "My mom has a copy of the play. Are you still using the copy on your laptop Jess, or did you buy a paper copy?"

"I bought the Arden edition with its million footnotes." I'd never read a book before where the footnotes took up half of each page.

"Good. So, we have two books. We can pull the play up on my phone for today for you, Damian, but we'll need another copy in the long run."

She was thinking in the long run already. What had I signed myself up for?

Evelyn played director. "For this first scene, Damian, you be Gloucester and Jessica, you're Kent. I'll be Edmund." As she said our names she dragged each of us into the center of the space in front of the barn. She handed Damian her phone.

"If you're Edmund you barely have any lines in this first scene," I pointed out.

"I'm being generous and letting you have them. But no, you're right. I should think long term. Jessica, you should be Lear, so you can't be Kent now. Help me out here, which characters interact least with one another?"

Reading the play and thinking through the implications of a three-person performance of it were two different things. I hadn't considered those details. I flipped through the first pages of the book.

"Umm..." I stalled for time. "Ummm... I think we need

each of us to be one member of Gloucester's family. So, if Damian is Gloucester, you and I have to be his two sons. If I'm Lear - and I really don't have to be him – then Edgar interacts most with Lear. No, wait. Both sons do a bit. We won't be able to do this."

"We'll do our best. We can't get it perfectly so choose – are you the good son or the bad?"

"I'll be the bad." Why not? I played the good daughter in real life. Playing an evil character would be a nice break from trying to do right all the time.

"Ok, then I'm Edgar. Hey – you're not just trying to get out of having many lines in this first scene, are you?"

"What? Why? Oh, no, that wasn't my intent at all. I'm thinking long term, remember? I've got some nice monologues coming up."

I went over and stood next to Damian. For the first scene Edmund, the evil bastard son of Gloucester basically stands there like a prize horse being admired and talked about by his father and his father's friend. I hated when people did that to me. Maybe that helped turned him evil.

It couldn't have been easy for Damian to read lines from the tiny screen of a cellphone, but he did his best. A few times he repeated lines a second time, when he realized there was some action or emphasis in it that he could play with. He had a sense of humor and playfulness. He wouldn't have cared so much for Evelyn if he didn't.

After the first thirty lines Lear enters, and I took up his role. After some discussion Evelyn agreed to play Cordelia, the quiet heroine, as well as one of Cordelia's evil sisters, while Damian would do the other sister. Each would play husband to the other's evil sister, and Damian would play both of Cordelia's suitors. The result was Damian having lines of two different characters right after each other. He took on silly voices to make them work.

When Evelyn's cell ran out of batteries and Damian was thus deprived his lines, we all sat down on the grass. I picked at bits of wild sage, rubbing it between my fingers to release the scent.

"You guys have been good sports," Evelyn said. "I thought this was fun and would like to continue this, but I won't resent it if you say you've had enough."

Damian and I looked at each other.

"I'm in," I said, "but I don't know time-wise. You have to work full time, Damian, do you have time for this?"

He was sitting close to Evelyn, but he reached out and pulled her closer. She put her head against his chest. Her hair hung down blocking her from my view, but I didn't need to see her to know she was smiling.

"If Evelyn's in, I'm in," he said. "Let's meet Saturday afternoon. I want to be away from the house anyway. My sisters' dad will be visiting." He wrinkled his nose.

Evelyn sat upright to look at him. "Rory? He's back?"

"He comes by twice a year to see the girls. He still flirts with Mom when he's there. He doesn't like my presence, so it's best for everyone if I'm not there."

I was calculating things in my mind. Damian's sisters were elementary school aged, and there were three of them. If they shared one dad, but a different dad than Damian, then he would have been a child with Rory as his stepfather – legal or not - for at least a handful of years.

"What was it like living with Rory?" I asked.

Damian had been looking at Evelyn, but he looked at me now. "He wasn't good to Mom. He yelled at her a lot. He wasn't that bad to me. He taught me a lot about cars and that has helped. He didn't mind me when I was a little squirt."

"What happened? Did your mom get tired of his yelling and kick him out?"

"The secretary at the town hall - I don't know if you know her, but her husband died in a car accident a while back and then she and Rory started fooling around. Mom found out and wouldn't stand for it."

I hadn't known. The town secretary wasn't in my parent's social circle.

Damian continued with his story. "He moved in with the secretary for a while, after Mom threw him out, but then they must have fought or something and he took a job in Calgary. He still tries asking Mom to move there sometimes."

"It must be awkward," Evelyn said, "your mom still living here and bumping into her ex's mistress."

"It's cheaper here than living anywhere else, and it's not like she has to visit the town hall much." He ripped a handful of grass and let the bits fall through his fingers. "People know the story. She knows people know, but doesn't know exactly who, so when she meets people she wonders if they know. It's probably part of why she stays home so much."

"My grandma put up with a mistress. She stayed married for my mom and my uncles." Evelyn spoke softly in a matter-of-fact tone. It didn't sound accusatory, but I thought the words might be taken so. I looked at Damian to see how he took it.

He stood up. "Rory wasn't worth keeping. Mom had been a single mom before, and he wasn't worth keeping. I should get home though and help put the girls to bed."

He started jogging down the path, but he turned back to call "see you Saturday," before disappearing out of sight.

# CHAPTER 17

# April 18th – 20th: Easter

My older brother was expected home from university for Easter weekend. He arrived a day ahead of time. Evelyn had her art supplies out on our living room floor and was sketching a picture of me.

I forgot about Evelyn's picture when I saw Chad. I just jumped up to give him a hug. "Chad, what are you doing here?"

"Hey there, little one" he replied, giving my back a quick pat before pushing me away. "Where's mom and dad?"

"Out," I replied. I hated when he called me "little one." I was sixteen, for heaven's sake! If only he'd hang around long enough he'd realize I wasn't a toddler anymore.

"Luke?"

"Luke is at his therapist's. Come and visit." I tried to drag him in to sit down with us.

"No, I've got people I've have to talk to. I'll throw a load of laundry in the wash quick and then be back in an hour or two when mom and dad are home, okay? Is there a roast in the freezer? Can you throw it on the counter for me?" He didn't wait for an answer. He just took off out the door. I dug the roast out of the freezer. Mom always cooked a roast when Chad came back to visit.

Chad and I had never had an easy relationship. I always looked up to him, and I was pretty sure he looked down on me. Still, he was my older brother, and the approval I craved from him could only show up those days we spent some time together, so when Evelyn was gone and Chad was back, I found myself standing in the laundry room helping him fold a load of laundry fresh from the drier.

"So, Sis, I hear your popularity has really taken off."

"Yeah, it ran right out the door."

"What happened?" he said. I knew he knew the whole story. He talked with mom and dad on the phone often enough.

"It's not my fault everyone is an idiot."

"Calling them idiots sure helps, doesn't it?"

I should have known better than to expect Chad to be sympathetic. I had to remind myself to unclench my jaw and stop grinding my teeth in frustration. I rolled two black socks together into a ball and tossed them into a Rubbermaid bin on the floor. "What would you have done?" I asked him, grabbing for another pair of socks as he smoothed and folded a shirt.

He shrugged. I could barely listen as he made some non-committal statement about talking to people, so that whatever he did do everyone would understand and be okay with it. It was a non-answer, a cop-out. My simmering frustration began to boil over. What right did he dare have to judge me for this? How dare he make it seem like this is my fault? I yanked at the socks as I finished rolling them and threw them angrily into the bin.

"Don't be mad," he said, grabbing at my arm.

I pulled away from his arm, but stayed. I was angry, but I knew if I left he'd just look down on me more. So, I stood there, frozen in the doorway.

"That friend you've got there – the one who was here when I arrived. Who is she?"

There was a topic I could talk about freely. I bubbled over with excitement until I realized he wasn't interested in what I was saying.

"Is she seeing someone?"

"Yes," I said, thinking of Damian though I didn't really know how their relationship stood.

"Is it exclusive?" he asked.

I rolled my eyes. "Bye Chad." I ducked out of the laundry room and retreated upstairs.

On Saturday Evelyn, Damian and I met at the old barn to continue reading scenes of *King Lear*. I didn't mention to anyone at home what we were doing. I wouldn't have minded telling Mom, Dad and Luke, but I didn't want Chad to know.

We celebrated Easter on the Sunday. Luke knew the Easter Bunny wasn't real, but we all had an Easter egg hunt anyway, because that was our ritual. Mom and Dad hid little chocolate eggs around the house, and we scurry to pick them up. At least Luke and I picked them up, while Chad pretended he was too cool for it. Mom and Dad kept a stock of extra chocolate eggs for themselves and Chad. They pulled those out after we'd finished the hunt.

Chad headed back to bed while the rest of us went to church. The minister had hidden a few eggs around the church for the children to find during the children's story time, and because it was a holiday there were a few extra children there. Luke didn't want to find any eggs though, so he stayed sitting next to me. Mom was probably relieved, because it meant he wasn't going to bump too close to anyone or crawl under anyone's legs while searching. He was better at remembering to give people personal space than he used to be, but he still forgot sometimes when he was too focused on his goal.

After the church service Mom made crepes with whipping cream and strawberries. It was one of those meals where there is never enough to satisfy one's hunger. I took two and then watched enviously, hoping I would get a third or even forth, but waiting to make sure everyone else gets enough. Luke used his crepes more as a plate for toppings, eating several servings of the toppings before eating the crepe itself. I wasn't sure how Chad managed to eat as many as he talked.

When Chad was around, meals focus on him. We ate what he wants to eat and we talked about what he wants to talk about. Luke complained sometimes that he doesn't get to talk about the subjects that interest him, but Mom and Dad reminded us that Chad isn't around often, and we have to make the best of the time we have with him.

Chad's newest girlfriend was named Barbara, but he wasn't sure how long they'd last. She'd hinted too frequently that she wanted to have kids, and he wasn't sure how that would work. She liked outdoors stuff, so he planned on bringing her out for supper when it was warm enough to go hiking, if they lasted that long. She was a vegetarian. He wanted Mom to be sure to have some hummus and pita bread on hand so she'd have something to eat instead of roast beef.

I was glad when Chad drove off Monday morning. I took the day off from schoolwork, since it was a holiday, and I lazed around the house. I debated calling Evelyn, but I didn't do it. Mom and Dad had drilled it into our heads quite firmly that holidays are family time, and you can't phone or interrupt that.

I sat at my computer and surfed Facebook groups for homeschooled teens. Maybe I'd find new people to talk to that way. There were many groups available, but at least half of them were highly religious. That surprised me. Most of my old classmates were probably Christian, or at least had parents who were, but we didn't talk about it. Yet there were teenage homeschoolers posting online about prayers and scriptures and how much Jesus loved them.

As I read further it became apparent not all of them believed in evolution or the existence of dinosaurs. I clicked away from one group only to find the next held similar voices. It surprised me. I didn't know people still doubted dinosaurs or thought the Earth was just six thousand years old. It kind of made sense that maybe people who believed that kind of thing homeschooled, because in school their kids would be told about evolution, but it still surprised me. There were other groups though, where the people didn't talk about religion or how young the Earth was. Not all homeschoolers were super religious like that.

Looking at the homeschool Facebook groups reminded me that there was Bible group for teens in town and that Madison went to it. I had gone once with her a year or two ago. We'd played some games, and someone had read some scripture and it wasn't bad, but I didn't think it was my thing. That group had been called "Teen Bible Club."

For local things, if they didn't have "Bible" or "Christian" in the name I would have assumed it wasn't religious. In the homeschool world online, it looked like things were the opposite. Groups that were religious didn't mention it, but there were separate groups that spelled out that they were secular. The default was reversed.

I found a secular homeschool Facebook group that looked okay. I felt weird about it saying "secular." I wasn't sure I counted, since I attended church, but I thought it looked more comfortable than the ones that didn't acknowledge evolution. The group's instructions said to post an introduction, so I did that. "Hi! I'm Jessica. I started homeschooling just a few months ago, but am interested in learning more about unschooling."

There wasn't much I could do after introducing myself. I read down a few different posts, trying to find ones I could comment on. There were some posts joking about schools and how they turn everyone brain dead. Would they think I was brain dead, having just left there? I wasn't sure. Later in the day I had some welcome messages. I didn't really know how to reply though. A few days later I changed my settings, so I wouldn't receive notification of the group posts. I effectively abandoned it.

# CHAPTER 18

# May 2th: Magic

On the second of May, Evelyn came to my house after supper and we baked brownies together. I knew the kitchen layout, so I had the job of getting out the ingredients and putting them away. Evelyn measured and mixed.

"Hey, give that back," she called, as I started to put away the vanilla. "I haven't added that yet."

I handed the bottle back to her. "Slow poke." Then I ripped off a scrap of the wrapping from a block of butter and began greasing the pan.

"Do you want to celebrate the summer solstice together, Jessica? I've been celebrating the Sabbats on my own, mainly with meditation, candles and poetry. I just wondered if we could do it together for a change. We could write out a plan ahead of time, probably by email since that would be simplest for collaboration, or perhaps Google Documents...."

"That sounds like fun. I'll try it."

"Oh good. I was worried you were going to think I was crazy."

"Haven't you learned to trust me yet?" I asked, leaning over to dip a spoon into the batter to steal a taste. She let me take some and then poured the rest into the pan.

"What shall we do as we wait?" I asked.

She stared at me as though I had gone crazy. "Now whipping cream, and chocolate sauce. You don't think we're going to eat this brownie plain now, are we?"

We texted Damian to come join us, and he arrived just as we were pulling the brownie out of the oven.

I dished four bowls. I knew Luke would want some, but I didn't want him joining us in the kitchen. I took a bowl to his room. He hardly looked up from his computer when I put the whipping cream and chocolate sauce covered brownie next to him. He had headphones on, but the cord dangled loosely from them. He wasn't listening to anything. He wore them because he liked the pressure on his ears.

"Thanks," he mumbled.

In the two minutes I had been out of the kitchen, Damian and Evelyn had started to argue.

"I don't care what you call God," Damian said. "My problem is with the idea of magic."

"It's not magic like magic tricks," I said, trying to smooth things over.

"He knows it's not that," she said, poking down through gobs of whipping cream and chocolate sauce to spear a piece of her brownie. "He knows it's not that."

Damian wouldn't give up. "What was it that feminist said?

Girls use magic because it lets them think they have power when they have none?"

"That feminist is Simone de Beauvoir," Evelyn took her cell phone from her pocket. I had the sense they had discussed the quote before because Evelyn knew where on the internet to find it. *"The idea of magic is that of a passive force; because she is doomed to passivity and yet wants power, the adolescent girl must believe in magic: her body's magic that will bring men under her yoke, the magic of destiny in general that will fulfill her without her having to do anything.* That's the quote you're thinking of, but it doesn't apply here. You know that to me, magic is about acknowledging that we have to set our minds to things, not just wait passively. You know that I'm not just waiting for life to fix my problems for me."

The last line was a stab at Damian, though I wasn't sure why. He recovered quickly. "I dislike the belief that the thoughts make a difference. It's like that stupid fad where people all think they're going to be rich if they open themselves up to the universe and they get to blame others for being poor or sick or anything, because obviously those people were attracting the wrong type of energy."

Damian had put his bowl down and was standing by the table, almost pacing. "It's like alternative medicine, where because we don't really have control over life people convince themselves their cooking spices are going to protect them from diseases. We're powerless. Why not accept that powerlessness? Why turn to religion to try to claim some power that doesn't exist?"

"So, you disapprove," Evelyn said, her voice wavering slightly. "Fine. I can live with it."

I watched her face carefully. She swallowed back anger, like I did so often in conversations with my brothers. I felt hurt and anger for her. How dare he disapprove so harshly of something that was so meaningful to her?

Evelyn wasn't done though. After a few minutes of silence, she spoke in a very calm, quiet, deliberate voice. "Religion isn't about changing the world," she said. "I know it can't change events. It won't make me rich or popular or keep me healthy. Religion – any real and healthy religion - isn't about that. It's about changing the practitioner, right now."

There was silence.

Damian dropped down onto the floor next to Evelyn and took one of her hands in his. "Just don't change so much you leave me behind," he said.

"Some gentleman," she whispered. "You know I have to..."

Damian touched his finger to her lips, silencing her.

The air in the room brightened. The tension was gone, for a moment. Evelyn let her head flop down so her hair brushed lightly against Damian's hands and her face was hidden. Damian twisted his neck to try to peek behind the curtain of hair to see her face.

"Gods, goddesses, circles of magic... It all sounds so strange and silly to me. You are such a smart, beautiful woman," he said. "I don't understand how you feel you need these rituals and such to make change. Heck, you don't need to change. But if you say you need these things, I'll try to understand. Okay?" He reached out and brushed her hair back behind her ears, guiding her head up as he did so. He leaned forward towards her. I wondered for a moment if they would kiss, but they didn't. They never did, or at least I never saw it.

I felt out of place. Things were too intimate. I didn't want to move but I didn't want to watch either, so I shifted on my seat, so I was turned slightly away and went back to devouring my brownie. In a moment or two the others returned to their dessert as well.

# CHAPTER 19

# May 4th: Joshua

Sunday, May the 4th was *Star Wars* Day. It was a made-up holiday promoted by internet memes and the vague similarity of sound between the words "fourth" and "force." The customary greeting on that day was "May the fourth be with you." Dedicated *Star Wars* fans had figured out how to stretch it into a two-day event by celebrating Revenge of the Fifth the next day.

Mom and Dad went to church alone that day, saying they didn't trust Luke and I not to greet people with the *Star Wars* day greeting. I smiled at the thought of Luke trying to explain over and over to people why he was saying it. We were instructed to have lunch prepared for everyone to eat together right after church.

While I cooked lunch, Luke printed out pictures of *Star Wars* characters and taped them to the backs of all the kitchen chairs.

My chair had Princess Leia on it. That seemed logical. I

could handle it. I glanced over at Luke's seat to see he had a picture of Luke Skywalker.

"Mom, you're Mon Mothma," Luke said, gesturing to her usual seat and the figure on it.

Mom smiled graciously and sat down.

"What?" Dad said jokingly as he gestured to his chair "No way am I Admiral Ackbar. I am not sitting in that seat." But he took his place anyway.

After lunch I texted Evelyn to invite her to stop by, and then I lay on the couch working on a few pages of my math textbook. I had only done a few questions when my phone rang. I dropped my textbook and papers to the floor and grabbed at the phone. I didn't think to check call display; I just pressed the talk button.

"May the fourth be with you," I said.

"Jessica?"

"Speaking." I recognized the voice but was sure I must be wrong.

"It's me. Joshua."

I wasn't wrong.

"How are you?" he asked.

I answered guardedly. "Good."

"What are you doing?"

"I'm studying math. What are you doing?" I didn't want to sound angry at him, but I'm sure I did. What was he doing calling me now, after ignoring me so long?

"I wanted to talk to you. I've been thinking about what happened. I mean, the police had your statements. There wasn't much you could have done differently. Trevor and

Martin kept saying if you and Destiny and Mackenzie and Madison had said you weren't sure who had driven the sled he could have gotten off, but I don't think that's true. I mean, they had your police statements from earlier, and even though the other girls were willing to say they weren't sure, it doesn't make sense. There's nothing you could have done."

"It took you this long to realize that?"

"It's not my fault. I mean, everyone here was saying you should have done differently, and you didn't need to volunteer to tell them about Trevor's other faults."

That got me angry. "I didn't volunteer to tell anything. I answered the damn questions."

"Whoa... I'm not calling to argue. Look, I'm sorry. I'm really sorry. I've behaved like a jerk."

"Yes, you did."

"I thought I had to, you know, go with what the hockey team was all saying. We stick together, but, well, hockey's over for the season. Imagine being in the locker room with everyone angry at me. That would have been hell. But and I've been thinking about things. I miss you and I realize you were right."

"Until the next hockey season and you decide you can't talk to me again because your friends won't approve?"

"It's not like that. Things have blown over now, for the most part."

"So as long as there isn't a cost you'll be friends?"

"That's not what I mean Jessica. I was wrong. I was a jerk. I should have stood up for you from the beginning. Give me a chance to try again. Come to a movie on Saturday. There's a couple of good ones playing in Fort Saskatchewan. I've been waiting to see the one about the spies, but I'll even go see a rom-com with you if that's what you want."

I was still angry, but I'd spent years and years of listening to Mom lecturing Luke on how even when his friends were wrong on something very basic and objectively wrong – like misidentify some type of insect – he had to leave them a way out with dignity rather than argue forever with them. Accept what apologies they gave. Believe the apologies even if you weren't certain. If I missed Joshua at all – and I did, greatly – I had to drop my anger.

I could hear a knock at the front door. I could hear the door open and Evelyn came in, peeking through the different rooms until she found me. "Sure," I mumbled into the phone in the long pause before Joshua started talking again. Evelyn was motioning to me trying to find out who I was talking too, and I was trying to sign to her that it was Joshua. My somewhat crude signs had her laughing, and I struggled to pay attention to what Joshua was saying.

"Sure." I answered again.

"Sure what? Which movie do you want to see?"

"The action one. I'm fine with that. See you Saturday."

I hurried through the details of when and where to meet - he'd pick me up at my place by about three; we'd drive to Fort Saskatchewan and grab dinner before the movie. Then I hung up the phone and turned to Evelyn.

"Joshua?" she asked, repeating some of the cruder signs back.

I giggled and replied affirmatively. "Joshua."

"So... What does he say?"

"He says he's sorry and he wants to take me to a movie."

"Are you going?"

"Yes."

"Good."

"Why good?" I asked. I reached across the floor to grab a cushion from the couch and tossed it at Evelyn.

"Because," she answered playfully.

I parroted back my old English teachers favourite phrase, "because isn't an answer."

She paused a second to phrase her answer. "It's good because you need it. You need to either go out with him and talk to him, or you need to get over him."

I thought about both those possibilities. "But it's fun to just dream about him and bad mouth him behind his back."

"Perhaps, but don't let it keep you from going out with other guys."

"No guys, Joshua or anyone else, would talk to me before today."

"You could ask Chad to bring some guy home from college when he comes next."

"Ewww, no. Chad has horrible taste in friends."

"Well, there's Damian. You could win him over by blinking those long eyelashes of yours at him."

The idea was ludicrous. First of all, my eyelashes were strictly normal, not anything special at all, and I doubt anyone anywhere would notice them no matter what I did with them. Second, and more importantly, I had seen Damian and Evelyn together. His eyes followed her everywhere. I was amazed he got any work at all done when she was at the automotive shop, but then I guessed that was the one place where it was her watching him. None of my classmates had watched each other like that. They might have ogled at one another, or checked out one another's bodies, but I'd never seen that constant loving gaze before. I couldn't imagine them apart.

Thinking about them being apart reminded me of something I'd been meaning to ask. "What's going to happen when you go to university?"

Evelyn wasn't sure what I meant. "What?"

"I was thinking about you and Damian, and suddenly I realize, you're planning on leaving this place. Is he going with you? Is he just saving up money now for college, or waiting for you to graduate too?"

Evelyn shook her head and began gathering up my fallen school work. "No, he's staying here."

"Why? He'd do great at university. He must have wads saved from working already. I'll bet he does go. Even if he's telling you now he won't, I bet he's just making excuses so that you don't feel bad he's waiting around here for you to graduate."

"Jessica, he isn't waiting here for me. We only met this past fall. He's here and he's staying here."

There was a finality to her voice. She didn't want to talk more about it. She put my school work on the coffee table and headed upstairs to my room. "Show me what you're going to wear on Saturday for your big date."

# CHAPTER 20

# May 10th and 12th: Two Dates

On Saturday, I wore jeans and a blouse. Joshua was late, but I wasn't surprised. Punctuality was never his strong point. I used to wish sometimes that I had the courage to keep him waiting, but I wouldn't have known how to. Being late myself would have gone against every instinct I had.

When he arrived, I was sitting in the living room with a physics book, trying without success to read. I saw his car drive up and had the door open before he had time to knock.

It felt strange to see him standing there. He was slightly taller than I remembered but just as thin. His Adam's apple stuck out at about the height of my nose. His shirt was untucked at one side. One hand was in his pocket and the other hand held his car keys.

"Hello," he said grinning. "Are you ready?"

I grabbed my coat from the coat rack. "Yep, I'm ready," I said to him, and then I turned and yelled into the house to Mom that we were going. I heard a muffled reply from another room.

We walked to the car. There was an old sweater on the passenger seat. I threw it into the back of the car and I settled in. The smell of the vehicle was comfortingly familiar, though I was impressed by the lack of garbage. There always used to be more junk scattered around the floor.

"You cleaned the car out."

"I wanted to impress you."

"I'm impressed."

The music popped on as he turned the key, and without thinking about it I flicked it off. Then I realized what I had done, and I reached to turn it back on, but he stopped me. "No, leave it off, if you want."

There was silence for a few minutes.

"I don't listen to much music now," I said.

"Why not?" he asked.

"Reminds me of old times."

"Old times?"

"Times before people decided that telling the truth made me not worth speaking to," I answered. There was a harsh tinge to my voice that I felt bad about. Joshua was trying; he didn't deserve to be snapped at. "I think it is that the old stations I used to listen to didn't reflect me anymore, and I haven't found new ones yet. "

After that we were both silent, but the silence wasn't the comfortable silence of old friends. It wasn't the silence I was used to, because both he and I tended to be on the quiet side. The silence felt imposing.

We passed the last house in town and I watched as the

fields passed by. I was beginning to wonder if the whole date was going to be one big, awkward mistake.

"What have you been doing?" He asked.

"Not much." I said, and then I grinned. I could say "not much" out of custom, but in truth I felt lots was happening in my life, and I was dying to talk about it. Nothing big was happening, but it's all the little things of life that make life interesting. I began to tell Joshua about those little things. I told him about meeting Evelyn and Damian, and about deciding I wanted to take charge of my own education. I thought about telling him about actually acting *King Lear*, but that felt too personal. I avoided mention of Wicca too. There was enough to say without those. I stopped suddenly, realizing that I had been talking for a long time.

"You've changed," he said. "You talk more."

"Yes, yes I have changed." I said eagerly. All of a sudden, I wanted so badly for him to understand how much I'd changed. I wanted him to know who I really was and who I was becoming.

"It's good. You're doing good." He said. He took one hand off the steering wheel and lay it over my hand, like old times.

I'd changed, but not so much as to make talking with him impossible.

The movie was okay. There were more needless chase scenes than I enjoy, but not much blood or gore. There were even a few interesting lines and a subplot with sweet romantic undertones. I savoured the romantic lines, imagining someone I hadn't yet met saying them to me.

The drive home was okay too. I talked, but Joshua was quite quiet. Afterwards, in bed, I realized that there were so many things he probably felt he couldn't talk with me about. Most of his social life was with people that weren't talking to me anymore. Was he avoiding any mention of that, to protect my feelings? Was that why he was so quiet?

Joshua invited me to come with him to the coffee shop Monday after school. I agreed. I hadn't been back there since the one time with Evelyn.

There was no one in the coffee shop when we arrived, but before my latte had cooled enough to drink, I saw a group of teens at the door. Mackenzie entered first. She saw me and smiled. She looked almost as if she might come over and talk to us when Destiny stopped her. Destiny was hanging from Martin's arm so hard I was surprised she didn't tip him over. "Something smells in here," she said dramatically. She pretended to look around before focusing on me. "Oh, it's her, I guess."

"Cut it out," Mackenzie said at the same time Joshua told Destiny to "stuff it."

"We can come back another time," Mackenzie replied. She pushed Destiny and Martin towards the door.

I didn't speak until the windchime by the door stopped its music. Then I looked as Joshua. "Are you going to get in trouble with them?" I asked.

He shrugged. "A bit. It doesn't matter. Mostly just a bit of ribbing."

I didn't know whether to be happy that he would endure some teasing for me, angry that he would have to endure it, or worse yet, angry about the double standards in the world that would allow him to have some semblance of a normal social life while still interacting with me while I was still shunned. I didn't want to feel grateful to him or feel his pity.

"You got to remember the good things. Destiny's not bad. She's really quite fun to be around and Martin's loyal. It's not like they're horrible people or anything."

Yes. Yes, they were horrible people. This was what Luke had talked about when he said the teacher told him how great his classmate Ben was. This was what Luke was upset about. How could any amount of fun or games or goodness out-weigh what they had done to me the past few months? What did it matter how nice they once were or how great they were to other people?

I knew if I followed that train of thought we would end up fighting, so I forced myself to change the topic. I asked him questions. What had he been doing recently? Any good par-ties? How was his sister doing? Was there anything interesting happening in school?

I forced myself to sit there listening to his stories, confront-ing my loneliness in that new way. It was like seeing how close to a hot ember I could hold my hand. How many stories of the life I used to have but couldn't have now could I tolerate listening to?

When the last dredges of our drinks, with the extra syrupy sweetness, had dripped down into our mouths, we left the coffeeshop and walked home.

I was glad when he walked me to my door and I could be alone.

# CHAPTER 21

# May 31: Draytons

Ever since Damian and I had eaten dinner at Evelyn's house, Evelyn had been pestering Damian to invite us over for dinner at his. At the end of May, he finally did.

Damian, his mother and three sisters lived in a small house in an older section of town. Straggly petunias lined the walkway up to the front door. A butterfly decal was stuck to the window of the door.

I rang the doorbell. It was answered by a little girl, her pink dress stained with a stripe of something orange. She stood there staring at me.

"Is Damian home?" I asked. Could I have gotten the day or time confused?

She nodded but made no move to call him.

I wondered if it would be rude to invite myself inside. Then I heard Damian's call from somewhere further inside house. "Come on in, Jessica."

I took a step closer to the girl. She stood still, and I began to wonder what it would take to convince her to let me in. Then she seemed to come to life, turning to run into the next room, her arms waving wildly.

I pushed the door further open and stepped in. Damian arrived at the door at last, a wide smile on his face.

"Elsa," Damian said, naming the girl who had just left. It was his youngest sister.

We walked through the living room. His mom, Mrs. Drayton, was sitting on a rocking chair, her left leg up on a foot stool. She had the same reddish hair as Damian. The television was on.

Evelyn was sitting at the kitchen table, chatting with Damian's other two sisters, Emma and Ava. They each had stacks of papers and an array of felt markers spread out in front of them. I wanted to get the girls to look up, so I asked if Evelyn was helping or hindering them on their drawing.

"Hindering," one announced, while the other declared Evelyn was helping. They both giggled.

Damian was at the stove again and then at the sink draining boiling water from a pot. "Put your things away," he said to his sisters, "and Emma, go tell Mom and Elsa that it's supper time."

Both girls gathered their papers and one, Emma, I presumed, shouted loudly that it was suppertime.

Damian rolled his eyes. "Don't shout. Go to them."

Evelyn and the oldest sister went to grab additional chairs from other rooms and I stared at the small table with five chairs crowded tightly around it already. How would it fit more?

While they were gone a fat, white cat jumped up onto

the table. Was it allowed there? Should I get it down? Could I move the beast? While I hesitated, Damian tossed a cloth hot mat onto the table and the beast made a leap down on its own.

"Sorry about that," Damian said. "We do try to keep him off the table."

Then Mrs. Drayton shuffled to the table, her left leg dragging painfully behind the other.

When everyone was seated Damian lifted a giant pot of spaghetti up over the heads of his sisters and dropped it into the middle of the table. A pot of tomato sauce followed. Dishing commenced without ceremony.

The girls chattered. Mrs. Drayton answered the occasional question put to her by Evelyn or Damian. I sat quiet for the most part, watching everything.

I liked the girls. They were cheerful, energetic girls. Elsa had decided to get over whatever fear of me had kept her frozen in the doorway and insisted on whispering things in my ear. The oldest asked me about my brother, whom she had some contact with at school. The middle child laughed frequently.

Damian and his mom were both always busy helping pass the food, grabbing paper towel to wipe something up, reminding one of the girls to eat with her mouth closed. The hot peppers, olive oil, and Parmesan cheese each necessitated Damian making additional trips up from the table as they were remembered and requested. The meal was chaos - happy chaos - but in amongst the business I wondered if I sensed some nervousness on Damian's part. He kept glancing at Evelyn and me as though checking everything was alright.

After supper Damian and I did dishes while Evelyn played cards with his sisters.

With my hands in the warm soapy water, I realized what question had been gnawing at me since the middle of supper. I wanted to ask him if he was embarrassed by his family. It was obvious he put a lot of work into helping keep the household running, but his family was definitely different than Evelyn's or even mine. Was it embarrassment I sensed from him during the meal? I couldn't think of a way to phrase it that wouldn't somehow imply that I thought he should be. He shouldn't be worried about it.

Instead I asked how his mom's leg was doing. Was she still in a lot of pain?

She was in pain.

"Does she take stuff for the pain?" I pressed.

"Yeah," he said with a sigh.

"Is there anything she can do to fix the knee?"

"The doctors told her she needed one knee replaced, but she refused. It's been almost a year and a half since she'd been able to work."

"Why doesn't she get the surgery?" I asked.

"There are a couple of reasons," he said. "Her naturopath says she can use supplements to heal it and her pastor says it is a matter of faith in God. Both the naturopath and the pastor make it sound like if she does everything right the leg will heal and if it hasn't, it is because she still needs to do more work to cleanse her soul or *chi* or whatever it is that stores bad energy."

Damian's voice was bitter. His college fund had been drained to help his mom through this time of unemployment, and his earnings at the mechanics shop were going to support his family. At nineteen he had all the responsibilities of an adult because his mom's beliefs prevented her from getting proper medical assistance. As he talked, I could start to understand a bit more why he was against religion and Evelyn's idea of magic.

"Not all churches are like that," I said. I couldn't picture the minster at my parents' church ever telling anyone to skip any sort of medical treatment.

"Her church is crazy, but don't tell her I said that."

"Why isn't she on disability?" I asked.

He shrugged. "She is, but it doesn't cover much."

My eyes darted around the kitchen. I saw his sisters' papers on the side-counter, the cat's food bowl on the floor, a small cross over the window.

I hadn't realized how much Damian did at home. Between work and taking care of things at home I was amazed he found the time he did to spend with me and Evelyn.

"I need an escape," he said when I asked about his time. "Evelyn's been my escape ever since that day she brought her dad's car in for an oil change."

I hadn't heard before how they had met.

"You've seen the shop, right? We don't have much space for waiting there, since no one waits. People drop their cars off and go off for a coffee or something. Evelyn didn't. She dropped her car off and sat there with a book. Not a cell phone, a book. When I was done with the car, I had to ask her about what she was reading. The next day she came back and sat there reading till I was done working on some stranger's car and had time to talk with her. After that we just started meeting up places."

I hadn't thought before about how lonely Evelyn must have been too, homeschooling in this little town. When she moved here I had heard of her, but I had made no effort to get to know her. None of my classmates did either. She must have been lonely. What might life have been like if I had reached out to her earlier? There wasn't a law that says that teens in school couldn't make friends with homeschoolers. It just never occurred to us to try.

We finished the dishes. By then it sounded like the card game had finished and Evelyn was the one in need of an escape. The two older girls were asking her to play another game; the younger was trying to get her to kiss the cat. Damian and I went into the living room, told the girls it was time to leave her alone. Then the three of us went outside to sit and talk till Evelyn and I had to leave.

# CHAPTER 22

# June 1st: Acting with Joshua

"You're spending all your time with Evelyn and Damian," Joshua complained. He had stopped by my house hoping to hang out, but I told him I was just on my way out. "What are you guys doing anyway?"

"It's silly," I said, "but we're working on acting out scenes from *King Lear*." It was a self defense mechanism to call the play-acting silly. If I said it first, it wouldn't hurt when he said it.

"Is that some kind of homeschool thing?"

"Sort of."

"Let me come too."

"We don't want an audience."

"Then I won't be an audience. I'll play a part. Any part."

"Perhaps you'll be the king expecting Cordelia to lie to him?"

"Touché. I deserved that," he said. "But can I be in it?"

I told him he could come with me, and we would see how it goes. It would be up to Evelyn and Damian if he would be able to join us more than the one time.

We were halfway to the barn when Joshua realized he had no copy of the script. "Can I share?" he said. "I'll look over your shoulder." He tried to put his arm around my shoulders, but I quickened my step and evaded him.

"You'll use your phone," I said.

The others didn't look pleased to see him, but they took it in stride. There was no reprimand for my having brought him. Since we had started, we had acted through the whole play twice, but Evelyn was insistent we keep practicing our favourite parts to gain greater fluency and understanding of the text. Nevertheless, we went back to the beginning, in honor of our new participant.

Joshua accepted it in good humor when we informed him that he would play one of the evil sisters for the first scene. It was a fairly minor part. He waited while Gloucester and Kent discuss Edmund's breeding. Standing there with my character being discussed felt more awkward with someone new.

Joshua entered the scene when I switched to playing Lear. As Lear's daughter, he professed his love to me to earn a share of the kingdom.

My favourite part of first scene was a dialogue between Lear and his advisor. Evelyn played the advisor, arguing with Lear to not lash out when his favourite daughter refuses to lie for him. The advisor knows he is stepping out of line in speaking thus to a king.

*"be Kent unmannerly,*
*when Lear is mad. What wouldst thou do, old man?*
*Things thou that duty shall have dread to speak*
*When power to flatter bows? To plainness honour's*
*bound*
*When majesty falls to folly...."*

I loved those lines. They were like a petition to hold fast to one's belief and speak it forth even when the person who hears doesn't want to listen. Speak truth despite risk of persecution. Kent loves the king so much he's willing to risk the king's wrath by telling the king that he is being foolish. It was something I couldn't imagine doing, ever.

I knew people probably thought I could speak out my truth because of what I said at Trevor's trial, but that was just me doing what I had to do. That was me doing what the law and my family and adult social norms said I had to do. It broke teen expectations but not those of the adults. I was still just doing what I was told, even if it wasn't what my classmates wanted. In *King Lear*, Kent characters go beyond all the rules and dares risk the wrath of their king.

When the heroine's two suitors enter the scene, we paused. Damian was used to playing both characters, but he suggested Joshua take one. Joshua chose the good suitor, the King of France. Joshua directed the lines towards me, even though it was Evelyn playing the heroine, Cordelia.

*"Fairest Cordelia, that art most rich, being poor;*
*Most choice, forsaken; and most lov'd, despised!*
*Thee and thy virtues here I seize up-on:*
*Be it lawful I take up -what's cast away.*
*Gods, gods! 'tis strange that form their cold'st neglect*
*My love should kindle to inflam'd respect."*

I loved those lines too, but it felt strange having Joshua read them as though they were speaking of me. They described someone rejected, as I had been, but they described someone whom having been rejected was then *loved*. Perhaps Joshua was trying to flatter me by addressing me instead of Evelyn, as he should have if he was playing his character properly. However, my own insecurities led me to fear a mocking element to it, so I hurled Lear's next lines at him with extra vengeance. It was probably unwarranted.

I didn't know what to make of Joshua. One minute it was like nothing had ever come between us, and we were still the friends we'd been since childhood. Then the next I'd feel this strange sense of uncertainty. I could still picture him standing next to Martin and Trevor. I wondered if he'd tell them about *King Lear*. Probably he wouldn't mention it, because he'd be embarrassed to have even taken part, but could he laugh about it with them? I wasn't sure.

I shook my head, trying to shake away the thoughts. He had apologized. More than that, he was with me, stumbling over Shakespeare lines for my sake. I should be glad. I tried to focus on my lines.

When we were done for the day Joshua walked me back

to my house. Mom was outside gardening when we arrived, and she invited Joshua to stay for supper. I don't think she could quite conceal her excitement that I was back talking to him. Her friendship with his mom meant that she knew all his interests and family news, so she knew exactly what to ask him to keep a lively conversation going throughout supper. I didn't have to say much.

After supper Joshua and I went and sat on the back step together drinking lemonade. I could smell a slight whiff of lilacs from my neighbour's yard. The lilac season seemed so short to me. I knew the smell would soon be gone, so I closed my eyes and breathed it in deep.

Joshua was staring at me when I opened my eyes.

"Lilacs," I said, as an explanation.

"I should bring you a bouquet from my mom's bush – but those are almost gone." His lilac bush always bloomed a few days before my neighbour's did.

"Next year," I said.

"Or maybe I sneak around to your neighbour's yard and fetch you some?" He put his glass down and jumped up.

"No, don't." I grabbed his hand, pulling him down onto the steps again. I would have let go when he was down, but he squeezed my hand, holding it. His fingers were long and thin, but his hands felt warm to me, and soft. I thought they weren't as calloused as Damian's – but I hadn't held Damian's to know. Certainly, they weren't stained like Damian's were.

I had turned Joshua's hand over in mine, and was looking at it as I traced the edges with my finger. I wasn't thinking about how intimate an act it was, examining his hand like that, until Joshua leaned towards me. He was going to kiss me. I knew it was coming and I panicked. I was thinking how stupid I had been when his lips touched mine. His kiss felt warm and familiar, but I pulled away anyway.

"What's wrong?" he asked.

I looked down at my shoes and at the colour of the wooden steps. The steps would need to be repainted soon. Chad did it last time, but he was away at university. Maybe I could do it.

Joshua reached out to turn my face towards him, to draw my attention back to him. "Shall I compare thee to a summer's day...." he said. Then he laughed. "That's all I know of the sonnet, and I don't remember what television show had those lines."

He bent towards me to kiss me again, but something about the expression on my face must have stopped him. He paused, searching my face. "Are you still angry at me? You are, aren't you? You haven't forgiven me for what a jerk I was right after the trial. Well, what, are you going to punish me forever?"

"It's not a punishment that I choose not to kiss you," I said. "I don't owe you anything."

He reached to touch my face with the tips of his fingers, but I pulled back still. "Of course," he soothed. "I didn't mean it like that. I just... you used to like doing this."

Yes, I used to like kissing him. I used to dream of him touching me all over and I used to worry about whether or when we might decide to go all the way together, and what that would be like. For a moment, I could think about that, remember those feelings. Some part of me still longed for him to touch me.

I wouldn't give in to those thoughts. I hadn't forgotten how he had treated me after the trial, but it wasn't just that either. I saw how Evelyn and Damian cared for each other, and I knew I didn't care for Joshua like that.

"We can be friends, that's all," I said firmly. I moved his hands onto his lap.

"Friends." He repeated quietly, tossing the word over in his mouth like he was tasting it.

"Friends," I echoed, "and if you say one word about being friend-zoned I will rip your larynx to bits and feed it to my cat." I tried to make it sound lighthearted, like I was joking. I thought my rejection might not sound as harsh if I could joke.

He put his hands in the air with mock terror. "Of course, of course," he said.

After a few minutes of quiet he asked what Chad was up to these days. Chad was working in a lab for the summer.

"Ooh, is he close to a new discovery?"

"He's mainly washing glassware."

He told me about his brother's summer job planting trees, and we talked a bit about things our brothers did to annoy us when we were young.

Then we said goodnight, and he left. He paused to look back at me. I raised my hand to wave, but was too late. He was already gone, around the corner.

I moved from the step over to sit cross-legged next to shade tree. I closed my eyes and imagined a great light swirling up inside me and then out through the air and soil. *Goddess, give me strength in all I do*, I prayed.

Damian and Evelyn agreed that Joshua could join us other times if he behaved, but when we set the date for our next practice he said he would be unable to make it. Instead he posted a vague note on my Facebook feed hoping I would "break a leg" leading to my great aunt wondering if I had injured myself and my cousins wondering what play I was in. I replied: "Nothing. It's an inside joke." I didn't want to explain about our play-acting.

"Joshua is out," I texted Evelyn.

"Out of what?" she replied.

"*Lear.*"

"Disappointed?"

"A bit. Also, relieved."

# CHAPTER 23

# June 9th and 10th: Acting with Luke

Joshua wasn't the only person to think I spent too much time with Evelyn and Damian. Luke was also complaining that I had no time to spare for him. On a whim, I invited him to join us acting.

"Sounds boring," he said at first. "Are there sword fights?"

"Sure, we can do the fight scenes," I said.

"Tomorrow," he said. "Not today."

"Ok, tomorrow," I agreed.

That night he had dad take him out to the hardware store. They bought long wood dowels, pool noodles and duct tape. Then they assembled some padded swords for us to use.

Evelyn and Damian were waiting for us on the grass outside of the barn.

"*En garde,*" Evelyn laughed with delight at the sight of the swords. She took one and challenged Luke to a duel. Luke insisted on spelling out the rules. Evelyn stood at attention to listen. A touch on the arm or the leg meant you couldn't use that limb. A touch to the body, and you died. Loss of two limbs killed you. Luke said he found the rules online.

"Our swords aren't regulation," he added apologetically.

"Because they're pool noodles and not steel?" Damian said.

"No." Luke shook his head. "They should be completely covered in cloth too, with extra padding at the end, and they should have metal inside instead of wood. Dad wouldn't let me cut his golf clubs down. They should be made with golf club handles. I showed Dad the websites, but he said these would have to do."

I laughed. "We'll be careful," I promised.

"You can't sue if you get hurt. I should make you sign something, but I didn't bring paper. You can't sue."

"That's fine," Evelyn said. "Hand over the sword."

We dueled till our arms ached. Then we turned to Shakespeare, reading only a few scenes. Luke did surprisingly well reading his lines. When we were done, we all lay on the grass and stared at the sky.

"What's it like being autistic?" Evelyn asked Luke.

My heart stops when people ask questions like that. I wait for Luke to take offense. He didn't though with Evelyn.

"It's like being in a quiz all day every day and the questions are written in a different language. I say one wrong answer, and everyone's going to be upset, and I'll be punished."

"What do you mean, you'll be punished?" I asked. Mom and Dad were incredibly light on their third child, I thought.

"I'll be punished. People will be angry with me. Sometimes they think I don't know it, but I do. People are always angry at me. If I try to explain things to people they get upset, and I'll get upset, and then I'll be in trouble for getting upset."

"You're scared of saying or doing the wrong things?" Damian asked.

"Yes," he said. "But not scared in the way cowards are scared."

"I would say not, since you have to face that fear every day all day."

"Besides, I'm rarely wrong," Luke said. "People just think I am."

Evelyn and Damian laughed.

"What's it like being an Evelyn?" I asked, trying to shift the conversation away from Luke before he could take offense at their laughter. It seemed strange him worrying all the time about getting things wrong, because when I was around him I often worried about saying the wrong thing and upsetting him. I hadn't thought about how much he worried about upsetting others.

"Being autistic and being an Evelyn are not equivalent questions," Luke insisted. "One is a diagnosis of a developmental disorder and the other one the identity of an individual person."

Evelyn and Damian both got a kick out of his specificity. I just rolled my eyes.

Luke had enough talking. He stood up and gripped a sword. "Who is next?"

Damian took the other sword and they began their fight.

I hadn't realized my brother was so afraid of failing. I hadn't realized how aware he was of all those expectations we heaped upon him. I had just felt the unfairness of the ones he heaped on us. There were times I was resentful about the extra help he needed from Mom and Dad. I knew I shouldn't be, but I was.

"Why aren't you an astrophysicist?" Luke said, taking swing at Damian with each word. "Jessica said you were smart. She said you could be one."

"Why aren't you a mechanic?" Damian countered. "I hear you're smart enough for that."

"To make an apple pie, you must first invent the universe. Carl Sagan," Luke responded.

Damian laughed and lunged for Luke's legs. Luke jumped to the side just in time. "Sagan's got it backwards, Luke. To understand the universe, you have to learn to bake an apple pie. You need to learn how an engine works, how gasses respond to heat and pressure."

Luke nicked Damian's right arm. Damian switched the sword to his left hand and tucked his right hand behind his back to continue.

Evelyn rolled over to look at me. "If you had one wish what would you wish for?" she asked.

"I don't know. Choosing one wish is harder than choosing three wishes. With three wishes I'd at least have two to waste." I answered.

"Why wish for anything that you wouldn't wish for if it was your only wish?" Damian asked. His head was turned for a minute and Luke swiped at his other arm. "I'm out," he said, admitting defeat. He dropped the sword and came back to lie down next to Evelyn.

I thought about what he said, about not wishing for anything you wouldn't spend your only wish for. It made sense, but there must be some mistake in the logic. The little things in life, the side-plots of sorts, had to be important too, right? We can want multiple things, and there's things that wouldn't be worth anything unless they came together.

"I'd wish for more wishes," Luke said.

"That's against the rules," Damian insisted.

"Whose rules?" Luke countered.

"What would you wish for?" I asked Evelyn.

"What can I wish for? I have everything I want right here. Friends... sunshine... love... peace."

"Chocolate. You could wish for chocolate," Damian informed her. It was a well-known fact that Evelyn was a chocoholic. "I'm sure you're just standing there dying for a handful of sweet gooey chocolate covered almonds." He reached to his backpack, thrown carelessly against a tree, and pulled out a small box. He opened the box, took some, and passed it to Evelyn.

"You are right," she said. "I could have asked for chocolate. Now I have everything." She plopped two almonds into her mouth with exaggerated care and then held out the box so Luke and I could have some.

# CHAPTER 24

# June 10th continued: Wicca

Evelyn texted that night with questions for planning the summer solstice. I hadn't thought much about what we needed to do, so I sat down at my laptop and began to google.

I giggled when my search turned up pages for midsummer fertility rituals. I forwarded a link to Evelyn.

"Ha, ha. Very funny," she texted back.

"How do we start?" I wrote.

"Circle casting."

I looked up rituals for circle casting. I knew Evelyn was looking them up too, and we took turns sending samples back and forth to one another. When we found something we were both comfortable with, we moved on to the next part of the ritual.

"Do you have a particular god or goddess to summon to the circle?" Evelyn texted.

"Not yet," I wrote back. Then I added a question I'd

been wondering about. "Gods and goddesses. Archetypes or spirits?"

I'd read before about archetypes, and the idea that the different mythological gods and goddesses represented some pattern, some universal character with properties that people could summon within themselves. I'd also read stuff that sounded like people believed the mythological figures were literal gods and goddesses. I wondered which Evelyn believed.

She responded with a one-word text: "Both."

After a few minutes, a second text came through too: "Does it matter?"

I hated when people respond with questions to questions. Of course it would matter, wouldn't it? One presupposes supernatural beings, one wouldn't. The archetypes idea Damian might even agree with! Believing without understand did not sit comfortably with me, but I texted back "I guess not," anyway.

When I had first been introduced to Wicca, I had hoped that a god or goddess would make his or her particular presence known to me and be my sort of guiding spirit. So far that hadn't happened. I had a sense of the divine as being a source of life, and in some strange way a connection to our backyard tree. The tree was a symbol of connectiveness, being rooted in the ground yet reaching up to the sky. I liked to pray next to it, and to talk to it, but a tree couldn't count as a guiding god or goddess, could it?

Hopefully there wasn't something wrong with me. Maybe I needed to learn a bit more about the different deities. Maybe that would help. I opened my laptop and began searching for webpages about the different mythological families.

After the sixth or seventh website I began to realize some of the things that were troubling to me. The first was that I wanted a deity to be a role model. Growing up in the church the emphasis was on how great and kind Jesus was. Was Athena a good role model? Branwen? Inanna?

I found myself reading a poem written by a priestess thousands of years before Jesus. The poem was about the Sumerian goddess Inanna and a mountain. Inanna, drenched in blood, declared war with a mountain because it didn't bow down before her. What kind of role model was that? Inanna stood in sharp contrast to the image of Jesus I had grown up with. Blessed are the humble, the peacemakers, the forgiving.

Yet why shouldn't the mountains bow down to Inanna? I remembered lines from Sunday School about how if the people were silent when Jesus rode past the very stones would express their joy. Maybe the mountains were supposed to sing out praise to Inanna. Maybe that was her right. Besides, the Bible had plenty of stories of God's violence, including earthquakes killing crowds of people.

What would it be like to know what one deserves and fight for it? Had I ever done that? Probably the bravest thing I had done was be honest in the courtroom, but that was just doing what I needed to do. It wasn't fighting for myself.

Maybe Inanna wasn't such a bad role model. Maybe I could hope to be like her, even a little.

I texted Evelyn my thoughts.

"Does a storm need to be a role model?" was Evelyn's cryptic reply.

I smiled at the image suddenly of Inanna as a storm, a force of nature. That made being like her even more appealing to me. But, Evelyn was right. The gods and goddesses weren't necessarily meant as role models but as recognition of the awesome power of the universe.

I sighed, closed my laptop and turned out the light. It took a long time for me to fall asleep.

# CHAPTER 25

# June 11th: Trevor

In the morning, I finished work on my *King Lear* essay, using information from the two library books as well as the insights that had come to me while acting with Evelyn and Damian. I gave the essay to Mom at our homeschooling check-in time.

"Very good," she said, after reading it through. "You said this is in addition to the stuff you've done for your courses?"

"Yep. I want you to let me do what Evelyn does. I want to pick out the topics I study and let me study them on my own. We can arrange for me to challenge the exams for high school instead of doing correspondence courses."

She flipped through the pages of my essay again. "Are you sure you don't want to go back to school? Now that Joshua is talking to you, surely the others will be willing to as well."

"I'm sure, Mom. I can do this. Please give me a chance."

"I'll have to talk to your dad. In the meantime," she put down the essay and stared across at the calendar on the wall, silently counting, "are you ready for your exams? Only five more days till your first one."

Mom had given me the choice of doing the exams at the school at the same time as my former classmates or doing them alone at the public library with the librarian as a supervisor. It had been an easy choice to make. We had the exams scheduled for a bit later than my classmates' exams, but I didn't mind.

"I'll be ready," I said. "I'll take my science books upstairs and do some review as soon as we're done."

We could both hear Luke at the door, coming home from school. I gathered up my schoolwork and retreated to my room. I had read about ionic bonds for about a half hour when my phone rang.

"Trevor overdosed," Joshua said. He sounded young and far away. "Trevor overdosed, and Destiny is blaming you."

Why would she blame me?

"The scholarship," he said, answering my unasked question. "She thinks he did it because he's angry he won't be able to go to university. She says you cost him his goals in life."

"That is beyond crazy," I said.

"I know," he answered.

"How is he doing?" I asked. "He got help, right? He survived?" It was hard to contemplate the possibility he might not have survived.

"He's in the hospital. We're all going there in a bit."

I wasn't quite sure who all he meant, but I assumed it included a bunch of people who weren't talking to me. It was strange to hear.

If it had been a year ago, I would have gone with the

group. Trevor and I had never been close enough for me to have gone alone to visit him, but I would have gone with the group. We'd have all pooled some money and bought flowers or something. I imagined that was what they were doing now.

I couldn't quite picture Trevor in a hospital bed. How would they get him to lie still enough to stick needles and tubes into him? But perhaps the overdose helped with that.

"What happened?" I asked. "How did he overdose?"

"I don't know. I wasn't there. Martin thinks it might have been a bad batch. Destiny thinks he did it purposely. I don't know."

"Was he alone? How did he get help?"

"He was at home. His mom found him and got him to the hospital on time. He's going to be alright. They say he's going to be alright."

"Are you okay?" I asked. He sounded so different, so upset. "Do you want me to come over?"

"No, no. I'll be meeting up with the others in a few minutes. I just wanted you to know."

I looked around my bedroom, then let my eyes rest on my dresser. "Call me when you get a chance," I said. "Let me know how he's doing."

I put my phone down and pulled a candle and matches from my dresser. Then I locked my bedroom door. *Goddess, heal my friend*, I thought.

He'd been my friend longer than he had been my enemy. Not a close friend, but still a friend.

Whatever delusions Destiny might have, it wasn't my fault Trevor had overdosed. Whether it was an accident or purposeful, it wasn't my fault. It didn't matter how important the scholarship was, it was his actions that lost him it, not mine. It was up to him to find a way to live with the consequences of his actions. But I would still care.

Cross-legged with a candle burning in front of me, I closed my eyes.

Luke pushed the door open. "What are you doing?" he asked.

"Nothing," I said. "Get out."

He slammed the door shut as he left.

I closed my eyes again. In my mind, I pictured myself summoning up a ball of light. I pictured Trevor lying in front of me, the light filling him. *Heal him.*

Mom made lasagna for supper. I offered to make a salad to go with it. I had noticed croutons and dressing in the cupboard earlier in the day. It has been a month or two since we'd had any of those in the house.

"Sure," Mom said. She set the table while I worked and then called my dad and brother.

When everyone had filled their plates and begun to eat, I told them about the news I'd had. "Trevor overdosed."

"On what?" Luke asked.

"Is he okay?" Mom's priorities were different than Luke's.

"He's in the hospital and it sounds like he'll be fine. I only know what Joshua has told me, and that isn't much."

Mom shook her head and took another bite of pasta.

"I've always said someone's going to die at one of those bush parties." That was my dad. He'd grown up in Toronto. Bush parties weren't a part of his teenage years.

"I don't think it was at a bush party. It sounds like he was alone and lucky his mom happened to find him."

"Corina must be beside herself," Mom said. "She won't want visitors, and I haven't talked to her since... well, months now, but I'll make some banana bread this evening to drop off at her place. People can always use extra food around." I don't think Mom had talked to Corina since the trial. If she did, I hadn't heard about it. Still, Mom believed very firmly in community and giving away food.

"Just no special brownies," Luke laughed as he said it.

Mom turned to him sternly. "Where did you learn about special brownies?"

"Television," he said. "But seriously, why do you guys care? Didn't Trevor basically destroy Jessica's life?"

"I'm sitting right here alive and well, thank you very much."

"You know what I mean. He's a jerk."

"Sure, he is, but we can still care about a jerk's family and friends, right?"

Dad cut in before Luke could reply. "Yes, we certainly will all care about everyone, jerk or not, and we're a part of this community. If your mom wants to bake some banana bread for them she can. Corina's done wonders with the school library and organized a fair number of those field trips you kids went on over the years, and her husband's the best doctor in town. I'm not forgiving Trevor for what he did to my little girl, but thankfully she's doing quite well now."

I hated when he called me his little girl, but he was right. I was doing well.

# CHAPTER 26

# June 11th continued: Mackenzie

After supper, I texted Joshua. "How's Trevor?" I asked.

"He's okay. Might be brain damage. He's treating it like a joke."

"You okay?"

"Yeah. Matt's just drove up. Going out with him."

I put the phone down and stared at my fingers. I hadn't been chewing my nails as much recently, so my fingernails were starting to grow out. I'd have to cut them sometime soon.

It felt weird being at home, knowing that there was drama going on. I wondered how their visit to the hospital went and who all had gone. Without thinking about it, I picked up my phone and dialed Mackenzie. I hadn't talked to her in months. I wasn't sure what she'd think of me calling, but I figured the most she could do would be hang up on me. That thought didn't sound as scary now as it had several months ago.

"Jessica?" she asked.

"Hello Mack. I heard about Trevor's OD and wanted to know how he was doing."

"He's doing okay. They won't let him out yet, but he was joking around in the hospital a bit." She paused and then added, "Destiny's blaming you."

"I know," I said. Her voice was very calm. It wasn't quite friendly, but it wasn't unfriendly either.

"Destiny's nuts. She's always been nuts, but it shows up more the last month or so. She's been so convinced Trevor will someday notice her and fall madly in love but as the days slip away she knows that's not going to happen. He'll be leaving soon."

"Will he still be leaving, even without the scholarship?"

She made a non-committal snort. "Probably."

I was borrowing Trevor's accident, exploiting it to have a conversation with a long-lost friend. I hadn't planned that when I picked up the phone, but that was what happened all the same. In another minute or two we'd run out of things to say about Trevor and I'd have to either get off the phone or see if she'd forgiven me.

"How's.... how's his mom doing?" I asked.

"She was down at the cafeteria when we arrived."

I nodded, even though she couldn't see that over the phone.

"What have you been up to?" I asked.

"Not much," she said. Then there was a pause and I could hear her taking a deep breath. "Look, Jessica, I'm really sorry for what happened back in February. We were all shit to you. I know I should have called you earlier, but after a while I just didn't know what I'd say if I called."

I choked up. She had wanted to call. That meant the world to me.

"Oh, Jess, are you crying? Don't cry. Look, I'll come over there right, now, okay?"

"Ok," I said through tears.

"See you soon."

I washed my face and brushed my hair again. I spent a few minutes tidying my room and then went downstairs.

It didn't take long for Mackenzie to walk over. She gave me a hug in the doorway, and then she led the way up to my bedroom.

Sandy had followed us into the room and jumped up onto the bed next to her. I watched as Sandy exposed her belly and begged for attention.

"How you doing, Sandy-girl? Do you miss me?" She rubbed Sandy's belly.

I was worried I'd start crying again, and I couldn't think of anything to say.

Luckily Mackenzie didn't need much prompting. "Can I tell you about the news from school? Destiny finally got her new car. Her old one caught fire so her parents replaced it. The way she tells it, the fire was pretty dramatic..."

Watching Mackenzie interact with Sandy, watching her get up and move about my room, picking up little items as she talked – it was all so familiar. Next to Joshua, she had been my closest childhood friend. She had listened for years as I complained about my brothers. She had turned to me through her parents' divorce. She had been the first person I told after Joshua kissed me. I had missed her desperately.

"...Destiny says calling 911 was different than she thought.

They don't just send the fire engines roaring with all the handsome guys. They had a lot of questions for her. They wanted to make sure no one was in the car and of course no one was but Martin did go back to the car to pull a propane tank from their camping trip out of the back. Imagine if that would have caught fire? He basically risked his life for her, but she still doesn't notice anyone but Trevor...."

# CHAPTER 27

# June 14th: Shopping

"Mackenzie's coming with us." Evelyn announced to Damian as he walked in the door. "Jessica has forgiven yet another of her so-called friends."

"Where are we going anyway?" Damian asked.

"Shopping," Evelyn said. "You're driving us into Edmonton, so we girls can get some shopping done."

Damian's eyebrows raised unevenly. He put his hands in his pockets and leaned back against the wall, like a cowboy in an old western. "Well...." He said, drawing the sounds out as long as he could, in a way that just reinforced the television cowboy image. "Just why am I doing that?"

"Because it is your day off work and you promised we'd do something together and I need to go shopping." Evelyn stood with her legs spread shoulder width apart, hands behind her back. If we were in a western, she wouldn't be one you would want to get in duel with.

"You sure that's what you want to do?" Damian said.

I could think of lots of things *I* would want to do with a boyfriend's day off work, if I had a guy as wonderful as Damian willing to do them. I wasn't sure what it was with Evelyn though.

"You're just going to make it hard for me to leave." She was speaking quieter now. Not quiet enough that I couldn't hear, but quiet enough we all knew it was directed just to him.

"That's not for a year away."

"One more year to get entangled." She bit her lip and took a step towards him.

He grabbed her by both shoulders and pulled her to him in a hug. "I'll risk it," he said.

"I won't. You just risk me leaving you. I'd risk deciding not to go. I won't risk that."

"Oh, Evelyn," he said. He buried his face in her hair.

"Ummm…" I said. "Mackenzie will be here any moment."

"Right." Evelyn pulled away from Damian. At the same time, he pushed her away.

"Ok, if you're bringing Mackenzie, I'm bringing Ava," Evelyn announced.

"Ava's not exactly the same as Mackenzie." I started. "If I was bringing Luke, then you brought Ava, that would make sense."

Both Evelyn and Damian glared at me. I was being logical, but logic was irrelevant. "Shut up Jessica," I told myself.

"Phone Ava," Evelyn said, holding her phone out to Damian. "We'll pick her up on the way out of town."

Damian wandered into the next room with the phone pressed against his ear.

"You have an amazing ability to forgive," Evelyn told me.

"I don't know if I could be that accepting of either Joshua or Mackenzie, but then, forgiveness isn't as big a part of Wicca as it is Christianity."

That jarred me. "I'm not trying to be Christian," I said. I was trying to be Wiccan, trying to open myself up to the Goddess and whatever deity might deign to guide me.

"You don't have to try. You are Christian, don't you see that? When you commune with the divine, you're just praying. You naturally turn to candles and chants because they're closed to what some Christians do. They don't feel as foreign to you as using rock crystals or herbs."

She had a point, but I didn't like it. I stuck my lower lip out in a pout.

"It's okay," she said. "There's nothing wrong with that. It's like you're taking the best of your Christian faith and applying Wiccan practices to it. It's fine."

Damian returned with Evelyn's phone. "Talking about Wicca?"

"Talking about forgiveness," I said.

"Forgiveness is overrated," Damian said. Evelyn and Damian might disagree about Wicca, but they held common views on the topic of forgiveness.

"Oh?" I challenged him to say more.

"Forgiveness means women taking loser guys back over and over."

That made sense. His experience was different than mine. He'd watched his mom be hurt.

The doorbell rang, but Mackenzie let herself in before we responded. "I hope I'm not late."

"Of course not," I said. I grabbed the backpack I used

instead of a purse and started out the door. Mackenzie followed me.

"Is everything alright? Do they mind that I'm coming along?"

"It's fine," I said, shaking my head. "Everything's fine. How's Trevor?"

She shrugged.

I threw my backpack in the trunk of Damian's car. Ordinarily I liked to keep it with me, but with five of us going the car was going to get crowded.

Damian and Evelyn came outside too, and we all loaded up. Evelyn sat in the front next to Damian. Mackenzie and I sat in the back.

"We just need to stop at Damian's house," Evelyn said, twisting around to face us.

"Okey-dokey" Mackenzie said with what looked a bit like a forced smile.

Mackenzie and I stayed in the car while Evelyn and Damian got out to fetch Ava. Ava was grinning ear to ear, walking to the car next to Evelyn. Emma, trailing two steps behind, was not so happy. "Why can't I come? Why take just her? It's not fair."

Damian ignored her until he was right at the car. Then while Ava squeezed into the seat between Mackenzie and I, he squatted down to Emma's height level and said something I couldn't hear. She appeared placated though not happy as she waved goodbye. Ava waved back.

Ava was small for her age with very delicate features. She leaned forward in her seat, towards the front of the car and her older brother. Her reddish hair was a mess.

"Can I comb your hair for you?" Mackenzie asked.

"I brushed it already."

"Let her comb it," Damian called back paternally.

Mackenzie fumbled in her purse for a comb, and Ava angled her body so she was turned towards me. When Mackenzie finished working through the tangles, she convinced Ava to let her French braid it. Somehow, even pinching the comb in her mouth while she braided didn't stop Mackenzie from talking.

"I braid my sister's hair all the time. It's frizzier than yours, but not by much. Hers is shorter. I think she should cut it really short, just a nice little pixie cut, but oh well."

Mackenzie tended to talk quite a bit, filling in any silences with chatter. Back before, when Mackenzie had been my best friend, I used to like her talkativeness because it meant I didn't have to work hard to think of things to say. I used to laugh a bit when Destiny and Mackenzie would both be competing to speak. I wondered how Evelyn and Damian were handling things. Perhaps I shouldn't have invited Mackenzie along.

"Are you going anywhere over the summer? I'm going to be spending some time in Vancouver. I'm not sure how long, but I have cousins there to stay with...." Mackenzie rattled away.

"I might be staying in Calgary for a couple of weeks," Ava interrupted, "with my dad."

"Oh? Do you like it there?"

"I haven't been there. Dad says it will be great though. He says he'll take me to the zoo, and we'll eat meals at McDonalds and go to movies together. But it probably won't happen." She sighed.

"I'll take you to the beach as often as I can," Damian said.

"Emma and Elsa too?"

"Of course."

"Promise?"

"Pinky-promise. Except I'm driving and can't."

"You keep your promises," she said contentedly, but the implication that others don't bothered me. I wondered how frequently her dad broke his promises to her.

Mackenzie had finished with Ava's hair, so Ava was free to squirm around more. When she leaned back she pushed into both Mackenzie's and my arms. The car had seatbelts for five, but not really the space.

We went to West Edmonton Mall and slowly worked our way through the clothing stores. Evelyn and Mackenzie tried on a few things. They found a few cute shirts for Ava to try on too. She was hesitant, but agreed to try them on when Damian told her to do so.

"Stay with Evelyn and Jessica, okay? I've got an errand to run." Damian looked from Ava up to Evelyn and I. "Is it okay if I take off for a minute? We'll meet up by the *Santa Maria*." The *Santa Maria* was a big replica of a ship in the center of the mall.

"Wow, he's gorgeous," Mackenzie said as Damian retreated from view.

I wouldn't have called him gorgeous. I thought he was strong, kind and very down to earth. He did have a nice smile.

Mackenzie wasn't done. "How did you land him? He looks yummy. Bring him to a bush party and I wouldn't need to be drunk to go down on him."

Evelyn, Ava and I all replied at once.

"I didn't land him."

"That's my brother you're talking about."

"We have children here, Mack."

Mackenzie put her hands up in mock protest. "Hey, sorry to offend, but seriously. Don't let a body like that slip through your fingers girl."

Evelyn took Ava's hand and walked quickly through the mall. Ava was almost running to keep up. Mack and I fell in right behind her.

Evelyn neither turned nor slowed her hurried pace she while spoke. "I didn't land him. He's not a food and you don't need to be vulgar."

"Sorry. Really sorry. My mouth is zipped." Mackenzie pretended to zip her mouth up.

Evelyn turned into a small boutique and busied herself looking at shirts. Mack went to the opposite wall and busied herself looking at slacks. There was still visible tension between them.

"I'm bored," Ava said.

"Look, I'll wait with Ava at the *Santa Maria*, okay? Meet you guys there in a bit."

The artificial lake with the boat was not far. We walked at a slow pace, stopping to watch water spurting from fountains along the way. When we arrived at our destination, I was pleased how much open space there was. I never liked crowds.

"It looks like it should be a pirate ship," I said crouching down next to her beside the artificial lake, "but it's a model of Christopher Columbus' flagship."

"But Christopher Columbus never came anywhere near here," Ava protested.

"I know. It's pretty silly."

"Adults are silly," she said.

"They used to have dolphin shows here," I said. "But that was a long time ago. Animal rights activists finally convinced the mall to ship the last of the dolphins out, so that he could live happily with other dolphins instead of all alone in a small tank."

"That was good, right?"

"It was good they finally closed it down," I answered.

"They did the right thing in the end."

"Sometimes it takes a long time to get to the end, doesn't it?"

"Damian said it took a long time for Mom to get to the right thing with Dad." She looked away from the artificial lake and towards my face.

"Do you remember before he left?" I asked.

"They fought a lot."

"It's been awhile since he left, hasn't it? It sounds like it is still really bothering you."

"He's always making promises and breaking them. He said he'd take me out for dinner for my birthday. He didn't. He said I can spend time with him in Calgary. I want to go stay with him, but he'll probably be too busy. But he promised."

Damian had just appeared behind her.

I nodded at Ava and then stood up. My legs were stiff from crouching.

"He called again yesterday," Damian said quietly to me. "Ava was angry about him not coming for her birthday, so he promised them all sorts of things. He told them about the zoo he'll take them to, the movies, the fun they'll have."

There was enough noise in the mall I didn't think Ava would have heard Damian, but she had. "I'm not going to forgive him if he doesn't let us stay with him this summer. I'm tired of him making promises he won't keep."

"It will be his loss," I said, "if he doesn't let you and your sisters go stay with him. You guys are so awesome, I wish you could come stay with me."

She turned back towards the lake.

We stood silently for a bit, and then Damian spoke again, quieter this time. "Forgiveness has its downside. Mom forgave Rory his misdeeds more times than I can count, and that didn't help anything in the long run."

Evelyn and Mackenzie both had numerous bags with them when they met up with us. "Lucky the trunk is so big," Damian said with a grin. He helped Evelyn carry her purchases to the car. I took one of Mackenzie's bags for her.

I watched Mackenzie and Evelyn. The two were speaking politely enough to one another, but I had a suspicion they weren't going to become the best of friends. I knew Mackenzie well enough to know she spoke more crudely than she acted. She spoke of going down on guys, and she probably wasn't really doing it. She spoke of getting drunk at bush parties, but she was generally a moderate drinker. There were others who weren't. There were those of our classmates who would drink beyond their limit and then bestow their sexual favours on whomever was near, but Mackenzie wasn't one of those. Maybe Mackenzie had been trying to impress Evelyn, sounding more sexually active than she was. Should I clue her in to how ineffective that manner of speaking would be for impressing Evelyn?

*Goddess guide me,* I prayed. My tolerance for being around people was wearing thin but there was still the long car ride home. I sat quietly staring out the window. As the telephone poles whizzed past us, I imagined there was a creature out there, not quite a monkey, but something like that, which could jump from pole to pole, keeping speed with the car. The image calmed and relaxed me, until I was willing to listen to what the others were talking about.

Mackenzie was still doing most of the talking, but Evelyn was arguing with her some. I was embarrassed, almost, by Mackenzie. Why did I invite her to join us? Why was she acting the way she is? She seemed more insistent, more crude, less able to gauge the flow of the conversation and what should be said. Her comments stood out a bit more than I remember. Had she changed? Or my perception?

Suddenly it dawned on me. She sounded nervous. Mackenzie sounded nervous and that made her eternal need to fill all silences even more pronounced. I wished she would relax. She was more normal when relaxed.

# CHAPTER 28

# June 21: Summer Solstice

Our summer solstice ritual started out with a picnic at the old barn. We shared cucumber sandwiches and a container full of grapes. Evelyn peeled the grapes one by one before she ate them. When we were done eating, we packed up the containers and looked around.

"We really should have a bonfire," Evelyn said.

"We can't here. We could have it at the lake." We could walk back to her place for her parent's car and then head out to the lake.

She shook her head. "It's fine. This will do."

All our play acting in the area had helped trample the grass down. We lay some candles flat on the ground. From her bag, Evelyn pulled out a container of sea shells and began to lay them out in a wide circle around us. I had a kitchen bowl, into which I poured my water bottle. Next to it I put my box of matches, and the paper on which we had our notes for what we planned. When we were ready we sat down and adjusted the candles so they'd stay balanced.

I struck a match and held it over one candle.

"I light this candle to summon the spirit of the Goddess Artemis," I said. "Wild woman of the woods, give us your courage and exhilaration." I still didn't feel any particular mythological deity was guiding me, but Artemis seemed like a good choice for two teenage girls.

I passed the box of matches to Evelyn.

Evelyn's voice was almost singing as she lit the candle. "I light this candle to summon the spirit of Ishtar. Warrior goddess, who will venture even into the underworld for her friends and lover, give us your courage and strength."

"The summer is here in all its glory. Time seems to stand still in the long summer days." I said, reading from our notes. "The plants are growing. Animals are well fed. Yet we recognize this as a time of transition."

Evelyn responded as we had planned. "The sun has reached its peak. Now the days will begin to shorten. Fall will come."

"We rejoice in what we have been given."

"We trust it will be enough for the days ahead."

Evelyn and I, each took a piece of blank paper and a pencil and sat and wrote reflections on the season. Midsummer is a time of transition, a celebration of the joy for the long days and a knowledge that the wheel of the seasons turns and darker days are coming. It was about celebration and the beginning of letting go.

Celebrating and letting go is an idea I knew Luke would hate. At twelve he still struggled with letting go of anything, but I was just starting to appreciate the idea. I wrote about the sense of joy I had at reconnecting with both Joshua and Mackenzie, but also about how I had a sense of letting go. I wasn't sure we were going to be close friends anymore. Letting go didn't make the value of their friendship or the pain of them abandoning me any less, it just recognized the different place they would have in my life going forward. Seasons shift and the people who are part of different seasons in our lives shift too.

When we were both done writing I opened my bag and pulled a small metal container out. It was a set face crayons, left over from a Halloween party three years ago. I offered them to Evelyn. She took a brown one and dipped it in the water. We had decided to draw symbols on each other's foreheads, and to make wishes for each other.

"I give you," she said, "the power of the earth. You are a strong, wonderful creative person, growing in the wild, yet grounded in the Earth." She drew a rune on my forehead.

"I give you," I said, taking a red crayon, "the power of fire. Dance to the heavens and beyond, Evelyn." I drew a small red flame on her forehead.

Then we held each other's hands. "Goddess," Evelyn said, moving onto the last part of our ritual - the closing prayer. "Thank you, Goddess, for everything. Thank you for friends, and love, and joy. Thank you for this wonderful world in which we live."

She paused, and I took up the prayer, trying to ignore the mosquito that had landed on my arm. "God, thank you for everything. Thank you for peace, and tears, and love. Thank you for sharing this wonderful world with us."

"The circle is open," we said together as we let go of

one another's hands, "but unbroken." That was an ending mentioned in many of the rituals we had read online.

# CHAPTER 29

# July 1st: Canada Day

Mackenzie, Destiny, Madison and I had a tradition to spend Canada Day together. We would walk down to the Canada Day celebrations together. We would buy hotdogs and watch the festivities. Most of the kids' activities were organized by Corina McNickel, and she'd have a signup sheet in the school library looking for volunteers. Sometimes we volunteered at the kids' games. Sometimes we would just go and gawk at the guys who volunteered.

Most years there was a fishing pond where children put fake fishing rods over cardboard and volunteers attached little toys to them. There were normally some tossing games, throwing beanbags or rings at targets. The last few years there had been bouncy castles. Everything was for younger kids, but last year Corina had rented Sumo wrestling costumes and a ring for teenagers to wrestle in. We had plastered Joshua and Austin's Facebook wall with pictures of the two of them dressed up in the fat-suits.

Every year, after we were done downtown we would hang out at MacKenzie's home, or mine, until the time for the fireworks. We'd walk together to the school hill, meeting up with other of our classmates. Then when the fireworks were done, we'd all stay over at someone's home. The next morning we'd make pancakes together.

I wanted to know if the others were all staying the night together somewhere. I had hoped Mackenzie would mention it on the shopping trip, but she hadn't. Maybe she didn't want to hurt my feelings. I didn't want to ask her outright because it might be awkward if she said yes, they were, and thought that I was fishing for an invitation to join them. I wasn't. I just wanted to know.

Instead I turned to Joshua and asked him if the three girls had plans for the day. He asked Austin, because Austin and Madison were hanging out together most of time. They were going to be at Madison's house. Destiny had been trying to convince Madison that Austin should stay too and if Madison's parents objected they could just smuggle him in the window and hide him in the pile of sleeping bags.

"Wouldn't the guys rib him for that?" I asked on the phone.

"Probably, but Destiny's got Martin convinced Austin should do it. Austin and I might go watch the fireworks in Edmonton instead. We can crash at my brother's place."

"That's sounds like fun."

"Want to come?"

"And crash at your brother's place with you? No way."

"You could stay at Chad's place."

"True. But I think I'll stay around here."

"Okey-dokey."

It wasn't a big deal. It was not like Canada Day is a big deal or anything. Spending the day together was just something we'd done for years. I think I might have started it because my parents always insisted I go down to the festivities, even when I didn't want to go. They said they weren't cooking dinner that night, just letting us buy things there, because it was important we support community efforts. I had invited the other girls to come along, and after the third or fourth year we started to expect it.

Knowing the day would amplify my sense of isolation from my old friends, Evelyn agreed to watch the fireworks with me and spend the night, but we would be unable to spend the earlier part of the day together. She would be in Edmonton visiting relatives and return just shortly before the fireworks. I hoped I'd get away with skipping the afternoon activities. Surely my parents wouldn't insist I join them.

At breakfast Mom suggested we pack a picnic and go for a long bike ride.

"Great idea," dad replied, putting down the tablet he was using to read the news. "If we leave within the next half hour, we could have an early lunch and still make it back for the festivities."

The point of the bike ride, for me anyway, would be to escape being in town and having to go to the festivities. Why exhaust myself with a bike ride if I had to do both?

"I'd really rather do some reading. I've got a book out on interlibrary loan I'll need to return."

"You've been getting a lot of books that way, haven't you?" dad asked.

"Yes, well, the library here doesn't have a great selection."

"You can skip the bike ride then," he said.

"Can I skip it?" Luke asked.

"No, you may not. You're coming with your mom and I."

Luke whined. "Why does Jessica get to skip it?"

"I'm older. That's why."

"I'm older than I was yesterday."

"Still not old enough, and I don't want to hear any more about this." I thought the tone in Dad's voice left no room for argument, but Luke had different ideas. He was still arguing when he, Mom and Dad finally made it out the door with a picnic backpack and water bottles.

"Good luck," I thought, feeling ever so slightly guilty that my staying was adding fuel to Luke's arguments. Perhaps he wouldn't have minded going on the ride if he hadn't thought it unjust I was exempt.

The house was quiet. Sandy curled up on the couch next to me as I read. After a while her purrs turned to snores. I put my book down and let myself drift off to sleep too.

"Wake up," Luke yelled at me.

"Let her sleep," mom said. Her voice overlapped with Luke's.

"I'm awake," I said, though my eyelids still felt heavy.

"You don't need to wake up," mom said. "We're back from the bike ride and we're heading downtown. You can come with us if you want, or you can stay here."

"I'll stay," I said, letting my head fall back onto the couch and my eyes shut. I might have drifted off.

It was quiet again when I sat up. The lights in the house

were off, but the light was still pouring in the windows. The clock on the stove said it was just two o'clock.

Homeschooling, I was used to the house to myself. I liked the house to myself. I liked the quiet. But somehow knowing what was going on downtown made the house feel empty. I changed shirts, hid a book in my bag and went out.

Even the residential streets were lined with parked cars, as I approached downtown. Two bouncy castles were set up in the empty lot the skating rink uses during the winter. The fishing pond and throwing contests were nearby. There were a few food stands in the parking lot of a grocery store. The hot dogs and ice cream stands were expected. The mini donut stand was a surprise.

I love watching as mini donuts are made, the dough dropping into the hot oil and floating till the big metal arm flips them and they float to the edge and out. I loved watching the cinnamon and sugar sprinkle down on them like snowflakes. I paid for a package and continued walking.

I could hear Luke's voice as I approached the park next to the hardware store. Someone had brought dozens and dozens of large cardboard boxes. Children were busy cutting, taping and colouring them to make castles and forts.

Dad was standing guard near Luke's castle. A small child with a cardboard sword kept charging at the castle, and Dad would move to block the child at the same time Luke would scream "go away!" Every so often Dad would put his hand on Luke's shoulder and remind him to stay calm, but I could see even Dad was getting annoyed as the child charged again and again.

"Not this fort," he said. "We're not ready for an attack."

There seemed to be no adult watching the child, but I wondered if one would appear quickly if Dad touched the child while trying to move the child away from the fort. I wondered too if I dared offer the child one donut – just one – on the condition he leave my brother alone. Would that be breaking the rules of human interaction to bribe a stranger's kid like that? Would the child accept the bribe?

The child broke off his siege of the castle, as an older man carrying an ice cream cone approached. The man gave the boy the ice cream.

"Mr. Cincinelli," the man said to my dad.

"Mr. Henderson," Dad replied, nodding.

The man turned towards me. "Miss Cincinelli," he said. "I am Mr. Henderson. Old Mr. Henderson, as I understand people in town call me. I was very grateful for your honesty in court last February."

I nodded, not sure what to say.

Dad stepped in. "Jessica just did what she had to do."

Mr. Henderson grunted but otherwise ignored my dad, still focusing on me. "Perhaps you think I was too hard insisting on the case being investigated."

"I don't know."

"Humph. Thanks all the same." He turned towards Dad and then gestured towards the boy eating ice-cream. "I see you've met my grandson."

Dad was quick. "Yes, we have," he said at the same time as gently pushing Luke towards the other side of the cardboard fort. To others it probably looked like he was moving to help Luke fasten some tape over the cardboard. I knew he was trying to prevent a scene. It was futile.

"He's a brat," Luke said as he spread the tape out over the edge of the box.

"Luke," my dad reprimanded Luke.

"I'm sorry," I said. It was instinct to apologize for impolite things Luke said.

My dad turned back to Mr. Henderson. "He's an energetic little boy looking to play fight. Luke is looking to build. It was conflicting goals."

"Very diplomatic, very diplomatic," Mr. Henderson mumbled. "And you, young man, defended your castle? What would you say if you were told you couldn't defend your castle and that you just had to let whomever wants take what he wants from it? That's what people wanted me to do when my snowmobile was stolen."

Luke put his hands down. "That's what everyone tells me to do! Everyone tells me not to fight back or make a fuss."

"Well, you can't hurt people," I blurt out.

Mr. Henderson spoke next. "Well, it seems you defended your castle from my grandson here without hurting him, so I'm impressed."

"It was mainly Dad who did."

"Don't be bashful young man," Mr. Henderson said. "Getting help is okay. I asked the authorities to pursue charges rather than punish the boy myself, right? You did good, just like your sister here." He looked at Dad. "You sir, should be proud of yourself."

Luke was getting upset. I could see him ball up his fists and grit his teeth. In another minute or two he might say something rude. He didn't like talking to strangers in general, but he was always particularly agitated if they tried to compliment him. He tended to respond as though there was always an insult mixed in somewhere.

I was relieved Mr. Henderson put his hand on his grandson's shoulder and they walked away, but I turned on Luke anyway. "You have to learn to behave around strangers," I said.

"It's okay," Dad intervened, brushing me aside. "It's okay."

"Can I have donuts?" Luke asked.

"Get your own," I said.

As I walked away from Dad and Luke, I reviewed the confusion in my own mind. Mr. Henderson had been polite and complimentary, but I found myself disliking him. It was unfair of me to see him as the reason I had been required to testify, but that was how I saw him.

Mr. Henderson saw pursuing charges against Trevor as self-defense. What about the other parts of their feud? Hadn't Mr. Henderson taken his own vengeance on the McNickels in other ways? I wondered what he would have thought if I had brought that up. It might not have been true though. It probably wasn't.

I licked the last of the cinnamon and sugar off my hands and crumpled up the mini donut bag before throwing it in a garbage can.

# CHAPTER 30

# July 1st continued: Fireworks

Evelyn came to my house around seven o'clock. We watched Netflix for a bit and then headed out around ten to the school hill to watch the fireworks. We went alone, since my parents were not interested in the fireworks and Luke hated the noise.

There were already a couple hundred people in little clumps here and there. Some were on the grass, but many had thought to bring lawn chairs or picnic blankets.

Evelyn began leading me on a winding route through the crowd, while I cursed silently. Any one of the clumps we moved past could be people who hated me. There was also the possibility of slipping or stumbling on someone. Why could we not just sit at the back edge?

Evelyn's purpose became visible. Damian was sitting with his sisters. We were greeted with squeals of excitement from

Elsa and Emma. They both crowded around Evelyn and she pretended to steal their noses.

Ava moved around to sit next to me, leaning her head against my arm. "Dad says I'll have to wait a few more weeks to stay with him. He says in August he'll have time."

"I hope he will," I whispered, though the sinking feeling that the planned visit might be put off indefinitely.

We sat quietly for a few minutes. I picked a white clover flower and pulled one of the petals off, sucking at the stem of each for the tiny drop of nectar.

"What are you doing?" Ava asked.

"Taste it," I said, offering her one.

She shied away. "Can you eat those?"

"I always have," I said.

It was then I heard the voices. Mackenzie's voice was the clearest, but I could hear Madison and Austin were there as well. I looked around. Everyone was blue in the darkness, but I could make them out. They had candles and matches. I listened carefully, trying to get a sense of what they were doing or saying. It sounded like Mackenzie had brought the candles. That was like her. She was like Evelyn. Both were very organized people, in their own ways. Austin was dripping hot wax on his fingers and offering to spread it on the girls, should any of them need some hair pulled off. Where was Joshua, if Austin hadn't gone with him to Edmonton?

A wave of longing rushed over me. As goofy and immature as they might be, I wanted to join them.

"Wait here," I said as I stood up. I said it first to Ava, and again louder to Evelyn. Evelyn nodded.

I knew I couldn't join them. I couldn't even bring myself

to walk toward them, but instead headed down the hill a little way to the side and then back up so I could come around behind them. Foolishness, I said to myself as I did it. Why didn't I dare approach them directly?

I was a few feet away, still unnoticed, when Trevor and Martin plopped themselves down between Madison and Mackenzie. They had four or five other guys with them, and a couple other girls too.

"What are you doing? You're going to start a fire," Mackenzie shrieked as her candle was bumped.

"Use electric lighting like everyone else," Trevor replied, shining his cell-phone light into her face and pinching her candle out.

"Hey, candles are fun," Mackenzie insisted, "and should you even be here?"

"Sure, I can be here. You can't keep a caged bird down or whatever that saying is."

Mackenzie shuffled to the side to give the guys more room. "Where's Destiny?" she asked.

"Off chasing that dog of hers," someone answered.

I retreated into the darkness, taking the same long path to get back to my friends. My courage was gone.


I imagined the fireworks were armies of magical beings fighting in the sky. I imagined the lights as a cascade of fairy-dust floating down on us. I imagined the colored sparks fading in the air turned into a magic blanket and wrapped around us.

The show ended with a waterfall of sparks flooding down from a wire strung between two poles. I remembered being amazed the first time I saw it, but by now it was more routine. Elsa, Emma, and Ava still watched it with wonder.

People began to move around us even before the last sparks had faded. Damian gestured to his sisters to wait. "Let the crowds move out first," he said, clutching Elsa on his lap.

I shifted so I was sitting facing him and Evelyn and the girls. Then I closed my eyes and just let the people flow past us like water in a river.

A small yapping dog leapt up onto my lap. It was Destiny's dog, a Shih Tzu named Walnut. He licked my face excitedly. Emma and Ava crowded round to pet it. Elsa squirmed out of Damian's lap, so she could let it lick her hand.

"Walnut," I said, sinking my fingers into his curly hair. "Good nutty-nut."

Then Destiny was standing over us with Martin, Trevor, and the rest beside her. Mackenzie pushed in front. She extracted Walnut from my lap and held him up to Destiny. "See, he's safe. He found a friend he recognized."

"He found a lying-no good - " Destiny snarled.

All three of Damian's sisters covered their ears. The younger two ducked their heads, but Ava stared up at Destiny, watching with wide eyes.

Damian was on his feet.

"Don't," I said, reaching for him. I wanted to disappear. I wanted everything to be over, to be home safe in bed, for none of this to have happened.

Trevor moved forward in front of Destiny, facing Damian.

Damian and Trevor were acting like our champions, like Destiny and I were two maidens in distress they had to defend, but that wasn't what I wanted. I wanted everyone to go home.

"Hold it," Mackenzie said, moving between the two.

Joshua appeared out of nowhere and moved to stand next to Damian. Austin joined Joshua, and Madison followed Austin. There were other boys and a few girls gathering around Trevor.

Evelyn was still sitting on the grass, pinned down by both Elsa and Emma clinging to her.

"Stop," Mackenzie said. "Break it up. It's time to go home. Everyone go home." She pushed the two sides apart and stood her arms out. "Time to go home."

Mackenzie spoke loud enough she drew attention from the adults and families nearby. I wondered if any of those there with their children would step in to help stop the situation from escalating to violence.

There was a pause, a moment or two of waiting. Then Trevor spread his arms out and laughed. "Sure, I'll go, we wouldn't want this little snitch calling the police because she's pooped her pants."

Damian tensed up. Joshua put his hand on Damian's shoulder. Damian let his guard down. He turned back towards us. He grabbed Elsa from Evelyn. He held her against one shoulder and grabbed Emma's arm, pulling her hand off her ears and drawing her up to standing.

He wanted us out, and quickly. Evelyn and I got up too, and so did Ava. Evelyn took Emma's hand from Damian. Ava was old enough I wasn't sure she'd want to hold my hand, but I offered it to her anyway, and she took it. We started walking away.

The whole incident had taken less than ten minutes, but I was in shock.

We walked to Damian's house first. His mom was asleep already, so the task of putting the girls to bed was Damian's.

"Wait till they are all in bed," he pleaded.

I nodded and sat down on the nearest chair. I was still shaking.

Evelyn helped herd the girls to the bathroom for teeth brushing, and to their bedrooms. I could hear the girls' voices drifting down the hall.

"Was he going to fight?" Ava asked.

"I was scared." That was Elsa.

"They were mean," Emma said.

Evelyn's and Damian's voices were calm and soothing.

"Sometimes people are mean."

"I wouldn't let them hurt any of you."

"There wasn't going to be any fighting."

"You're home safe, safe and sound."

Evelyn came and sat across from me. "Damian's going to wait with Elsa," she said. "You don't mind us waiting here?"

I shook my head. I wasn't in a rush to go to bed. I wouldn't be able to fall asleep for hours. The house felt warm and cozy, and as good a place as any to wait. There was clutter every-where, but none of that mattered.

"That was sure something," she said, looking at me in-tensely.

That was when I broke down. Everything came pouring out of me. "I can't. That was awful. I'm so sorry. They wouldn't have done that if I wasn't with you. It was my fault.

I shouldn't be with you. I shouldn't be with anyone. I just can't... I don't know what I can do..."

"It's okay. It's okay sweetie. It's not your fault." She moved to sit next to me, to wrap her arms around me. "It's okay," she crooned.

"I can't... I can't... I don't know what to do. They're going to be like that till I move. I can't..."

"It's okay."

I kept babbling, and she kept comforting me.

Down the hall a door shut. There were quiet footsteps and another door opened. Damian was talking to Ava now. "Ava, I'm going to drive Evelyn and Jessica home. I'll be back in a little bit. The door will be locked, and you can wake Mom if you really need. You won't need her though."

I couldn't make out what Ava answered, but Damian came into living room. He crouched down on the floor, so he was eye level with me, like he did when he was talking to one of his sisters. I looked away and wiped at the tears with my arm.

"Let's get you home," he said, pulling his keys out and locking the door behind him as left.

Evelyn sat in the back of the car with me. She wrapped her arm around my shoulder again, and I leaned against hers.

"I'm so sorry your sisters had to witness that," I said. I struggled to keep myself calm. I didn't want to start blubbering again. I just wanted to apologize. His sisters shouldn't have had to see that.

"None of that was your fault, Jessica. Not one little bit of that was your fault."

It still felt like the fault was all mine.

I fumbled with the car door trying to get out. Damian hopped out and opened it for me.

"Are you going to be okay?" Evelyn asked, climbing out of the car.

I forced myself to take a deep breath. I wanted to sound confident, even though I wasn't.

"I'm going to be okay."

Evelyn gave me a hug and moved around to the front seat of the car. They didn't drive off till I had unlocked the door and gone inside. I locked the door behind me.

I still felt like I could collapse on the floor, but I didn't. I poured myself a glass of milk and pulled a bag of chocolate chips out of the cupboard. I poured myself a handful, not bothering to clean up the few that dropped down onto the floor. I stuffed them into my mouth, drank the milk, and took another handful of chocolate chips. Then I walked upstairs to bed. I left the lights in the kitchen on behind me.

I wrapped myself tight in the blankets and revisited everything in my mind. I wish Damian would have sat down. He could have kept quiet. Destiny could have thrown her insults at me and I would have just absorbed them, and we wouldn't have had to worry that things could have turned to violence. Yet one couldn't ask a guy like Damian to just stand down. And hadn't I wanted Joshua to defend me when the school had turned against me? Yet here Damian did what Joshua had failed to, and I was angry at him for doing so. It wasn't fair. Nothing was fair about it, and everything confused me.

# CHAPTER 31

# July 2nd: Canoeing

The next day Evelyn texted me to meet her at her place. She said the three of us – she, Damian and I – were going canoeing. She had arranged with Gary for Damian to have the day off work. While we loaded the lifejackets and paddles into the car, Damian asked Evelyn how she had managed that.

"Magic," Evelyn said, flicking her wrist to cast a pretend firebolt at him.

He ignored the firebolt and rolled his eyes at the comment.

"Evelyn's charming," I said trying to keep everything light. "Gary can't resist her charms."

Evelyn scrunched up her face. "Ewww, that makes it sound like I prostituted myself. I just asked him very politely."

"Well, I am grateful," he said. He bent down and kissed her forehead quickly. She brushed him away.

We strapped Evelyn's parents canoe to Damian's car and drove to Miroque Lake. We turned off the gravel road, onto the smaller winding road that we had walked back in March. It was sandy, with deep ruts where vehicles had driven before.

We parked about a hundred meters from the lake. Evelyn and Damian unloaded the canoe and carried it down to the lake. I hauled all three life-jackets and the paddles.

"Which of you is paddling?" Evelyn asked, offering one of the paddles in our direction. Those in the front and back of the canoe would have to paddle. Whomever was in the middle would be able to just rest.

I looked at Damian. "You can, if you want," I said.

"No, I'm fine. I'll be the supercargo," he answered.

"Supercargo?"

"The head honcho in charge of selling merchandise," he said, smiling. "The one the crew and captain view as an annoying inconvenience."

Evelyn laughed. "He means he wants to play lazy-bones. Watch. He'll be asleep in no time."

Evelyn stood at the edge of the lake with her legs on either side of the canoe, holding it steady. I held onto the edges with both hands as I climbed in. I settled myself in the white plastic seat at the front of the canoe. Damian climbed in next, sitting cross-legged on the floor. Evelyn pushed off and jumped in.

I had canoed a handful of times with Joshua's family. The last of those times had been a few years back but paddling felt comfortable and familiar. I didn't have to worry about steering. Evelyn would do that from the back.

The water was still and beautiful in front of me. The hills around the lake were all covered in trees, mostly pine and spruce but with patches of birch. The lake had looked small to me, but as we reached what I had thought was the end I could see the lake bent around the hill and we could continue further.

We crossed the next section of lake quickly, and again as we reached the apparent end we could see around a bend into a third area. In this section the edges of the lake were filled with reeds. Two Canadian geese took off into the air, squawking as we approached.

Evelyn steered us along the east edge of the lake, close to the reeds until she found what she was looking for. The reeds were matted together, but there was a narrow path between them.

"It's a beaver path," she said.

"It's too narrow. We can't go through."

"Sure, we can."

We inched forward bit by bit. We couldn't paddle anymore, just spear at the reeds and push. Damian sat up and grabbed at big tufts of reeds ahead of him and then pulled to force the canoe forward.

"Dead end," I announced, as the beaver path ended at a beaver dam. The dam was low, only about the same height as the top of the reeds. Most of the bare branches sticking from it were grey with age but a few were fresh and yellowish-looking.

"Up and over," Evelyn said.

I twisted in my seat to look back at her. "You've got to be kidding."

"Just a second. Let me get out of the canoe." Damian began to move forward, hunched over and reaching to the side to get out. The canoe rocked precariously. Even with the matted reeds on both sides, I thought we'd still be able to tip if he wasn't careful.

"Wait, I'll get out," I said. My climbing out the front would be safer than him getting out the side. I could do it without tipping things. I climbed up onto the muddy dam and then shifted to the side so he could get out too. I looked over the area directly in front of the canoe. There were no branches sticking out right there. Maybe we could do this.

With only Evelyn in the canoe it was back-heavy, with the front tipping out of the water. Damian and I grabbed the sides and began to pull. I cringed at the sound of the canoe scraping along the dam. Soon Evelyn, still in the canoe, was right next to us, with the front three-quarters of the canoe sticking up over the dam. Water was seeping into my shoes. The sticks, reeds and mud beneath me were sinking under my weight. The poor beaver would have to do some repairs after we left.

"Ready?" I said.

"Ready," Damian answered. "Let's get this beast over."

We pulled the back section of the canoe up and shoved it over the edge. The canoe bobbed a bit and shot a few feet into the open lake beyond the dam. Evelyn paddled it around so that the front was facing us and we could climb in, Damian first and then me.

Behind the dam was one last small section of lake. We slowly paddled along the shore. Redwing blackbirds sung from the tree tops. The water smelled worse to me here, and I looked down trying to gauge the depth.

"A fish. I saw a fish!"

"My dad and I found this place the first summer we moved

here," Evelyn said, "The reeds have grown in quite a bit. I wasn't sure we were going to make it through."

"You weren't sure? You told us we could do it," I said.

"I hoped. I was right though, wasn't I?"

I dipped my paddle into the water and then swung it quickly back to splash her.

"Hey, I didn't do anything," Damian said when the water hit him.

"Friendly-fire. You were in the way."

It felt like there was a good possibility he would retaliate with some splashes my way, and I braced myself for that, but Evelyn's voice cut through our goofiness. "I love this place. I love secret, private places. Even though the whole of the lake is wonderfully private, this part just feels ever so more secret therefore magical."

"You'll miss this when you move away," Damian said.

"I'll come visit. This is my sacred lake. If I believed in the sort of magic that fairytales are filled with, I would believe mermaids make their home here. Or that the beavers here somehow hold the world together with their dam. A dam isn't just a thing that's built and then left, you know. They have to do ongoing maintenance, or it will fall apart, like everything else in our life, decaying under use and entropy."

"We should have been more careful with the dam then, we wouldn't want the universe to fall apart as a result of our canoe trip," Damian said keeping his face as straight as he could.

"I know you laugh at me behind my back," she said. "I know you don't understand the fantasies I have about places."

I cut in. "I do understand. I imagine all sorts of things too."

It shouldn't have been so hard to say that, but it was. I didn't want Damian to think less of me, and I thought he might. His love for Evelyn let him overlook a lot of her childish exuberance, but it wouldn't protect his good opinion of me. Still, I didn't want Evelyn to think she was alone and I wanted to have the courage to say my piece. "I imagine... well... castles in the sky really, in the clouds. When I go skiing with my family, I still imagine the mountains as sleeping giants."

"Hey, I'm not bashing imagination," Damian said. "I had lots of it."

"Right. Before you became an old man."

"Hey, I'm not old. Don't you go calling me old."

I knew why Damian didn't like being called old. He was two years older than Evelyn. Now if Destiny or Madison or half of my other classmates were dating someone older than them they would gloat about the age difference. They would see it as a sign of prestige to be liked by someone older, but Evelyn didn't see things that way. She liked him, but the fact he had graduated and stayed in town wasn't something she was impressed with. She would probably have been happier if he was still in school, getting ready to leave for university soon. She wanted to keep imagining he was another student, not an adult tied to the town, and Damian didn't want to disturb that vision of hers. He hated when anyone referred to his age.

The whole thing was so unfair. It wasn't as if Damian was just being lazy, or as though he lacked ambition. He had ambition, he just wasn't willing to change it at the expense of his family, and they needed him.

When we circled back around to the beaver's dam, Damian

and I got out again to pull the canoe over. Then we traded spots, so I could sit in the middle daydreaming on the way home, while Damian could stretch his muscles.

# CHAPTER 32

# July 9th: Mom

"I need a pair of scissors," Luke announced. He looked like he had dipped his hands in white glue. The glue was drying, and he was peeling it off leaving little bits all over the carpet. "I need a pair of scissors," he repeated.

"So?" I was lying on the couch reading.

"I can't find one."

"There's one in the corner drawer in the kitchen."

"No there isn't. I looked."

"I might have used it in my room. Check on the night table."

Luke stomped off upstairs. I returned to my book. He came back with his hands behind his back.

"Did you find the scissors?" I asked.

"Yes. I found this too." He held out a book on Wicca.

"Give that to me," I said, reaching for it. He pulled it back. I sat up on the couch. "Give it to me," I said again.

He stood there anyway. "It's on witchcraft," he said.

"Luke," I said. It was like coaxing a squirrel. I knew if I moved too quick he would dart off. I needed to lure him in. "I know the book looks strange. You're wondering why I have a book on witchcraft. The book isn't what you think it is. It isn't about something bad or scary. I want you to come and give me the book."

I put out my hand. He hesitated and then gave me the book. I put the book on my lap and folded my hands across it.

"I have to tell Mom," he said.

"No, Luke. Look, you don't have to tell her anything. There's nothing wrong with the book. There's nothing wrong with my having it but if you tell her about it she's going to ask lots of questions."

"Are you asking me to lie for you?" Luke visibly stiffened. He was impeccably honest.

"Not lie. Just don't mention it. Show me what craft you've been working on."

For a moment, I had hope he'd accept my changing the topic. He stopped picking at the glue on his fingers and looked up at me. Then we could hear mom opening the door, coming in from the garden. Luke dashed forward, pulled the book out from under my hands.

"I'm giving it to Mom," he said as left the room.

I heard Luke collide into Mom in the hall.

"Slow down," she said. "You've got to watch where you're going. No, don't give me anything. My hands are dirty still."

She went to the bathroom sink to scrub her hands off. Luke waited by the door. I could go and tackle him for the book, but he'd tell her about it anyway. I just waited. I heard her send Luke off to work on his craft before she came into the living room.

"Jessica, what's this about?" Mom asked. Her face was an unrevealing mask but her voice had a harsh note to it.

We sat together on the couch to discuss it. She at one end of the couch and I at the other. The book sat there on the cushion in between us.

Mom pursed her lips. "Maybe you should talk to Rev. Rickson."

An image of sitting in his office across from him flashed in my mind. That would be awkward. I wouldn't know what to say and I didn't want to try talking to him.

"What would be the point of that mom? Are you wanting me to sit there and listen to a lecture on how I'm wrong on this and it is dangerous?"

"Is that what you think he would tell you?"

I pictured the reverend with his white robes and rotation of coloured stoles. He talked frequently about interfaith dialogue, though I know he was meaning specifically with Judaism and Islam, since those are two groups Christianity had harmed. He probably meant native spirituality too though, since the church had apologized for their role in the residential schools, where native children had been taught Christianity and abused. I didn't think he'd have a problem with Buddhism or Hinduism either.

"I don't know what he'd say. Maybe he'd say it is wrong, or maybe he'd recognize it as another path to God, but wouldn't that depend almost entirely on how familiar he is with Wicca? He might... he might be the expert on Christianity, but we don't know if he knows anything about Wicca."

She picked up the book, turned it over and over in her hands and then began tapping it against the couch. "Should I read this?"

I thought for a minute before answering. "You could, but it only gives the views of that one author. I'm not sure how much I agree with it."

Mom liked that response. "I guess it is your views that are more important than what that author believes."

I was annoyed that Mom wanted to probe inside my mind. Why should I have to justify my faith to her? I was almost seventeen. I should be allowed to have my own beliefs.

She seemed to have dropped the idea of my talking to Rev. Rickson, and she wasn't threatening to cut off my internet or ban me from reading books on Wicca or anything like that. She'd never been one to ground us kids either. So maybe she wasn't really trying to control my thoughts. I didn't know. Why couldn't she leave me alone?

I thought about what Evelyn had said at the summer solstice, about how I had seemed more Christian than Wiccan anyway. I had felt insulted at the time, but maybe she was right. I took a deep breath and attempted to explain.

"Mom, you taught me to love God. You taught me to believe in Jesus, but you also taught me that Jesus isn't the only way in which God has spoken to the world. God has reached out to the world and called people into communion with him in so many different forms. Modern paganism draws on the myths and stories of older times, of people struggling to make sense of God and God's world in other ways."

"Oh, Jess...."

I was laying the connection with Christianity a bit stronger than I felt, but I wanted to reassure mom. I tried to take a step back and just talk from the heart.

"My thoughts aren't that different now. I still believe that God is a loving, guiding force within the world. I still believe in truth and honesty, in love, in trying to serve the divine light. I just think that God is trying to reach me in other ways, to talk to me outside of church as well as in it."

"Is it the same God though, in Wicca?" she asked.

"If there is only one God, how can it not be?" I countered.

She paused, reflecting on the question, so I expanded on my own ideas. "I think, there might be different ways of picturing the one God. The ideas probably aren't all equal. A hateful God is not equal to a loving God. Yet, there are Christians who worship a God that would torture souls in eternity. There are Christians who worship a hateful God. I think that I can find a way to worship a loving God, within the practices of Wicca."

"Is it worshipping in the wrong way?" she asked.

"People have worshipped in all different ways throughout history, haven't they?"

We talked for over an hour, and Mom was still skeptical by the end. She said she needed more time to think about it all and she was concerned that I hadn't told her about my new interest myself. Hiding things, she said, seems like an admission of wrongdoing. That was another whole point of contention.

"I wasn't hiding them," I protested vainly. "I just didn't think you needed to know my every thought and action."

Mom looked for a moment like she might reply to that,

but instead she left to make supper, and I took the opportunity to retreat to my own room.

I felt shaken. I hadn't wanted to argue with Mom about the whole thing. I wasn't trying to hide it out of guilt or fear. Keeping it to myself had felt special. It was sacred. I had pictured Luke and Dad approaching it with the same skepticism Damian had and didn't want to open it up to their criticism. I had forgotten to think of how Mom, with her own deep religious convictions, might feel.

As I thought over the conversation, I could feel my annoyance rising. What business was it of hers what I believed? Yet even as that thought bubbled up, another replaced it. She only meant the best. She cared. I'd probably be concerned too, if I was a parent whose child started into some new religion.

That evening Luke came to my bedroom and stood in the doorway, shifting from side to side. "Are you in trouble? Am I in trouble?"

He was wearing his favourite grey sweatpants and a bright red shirt. He was looking at the floor.

"You didn't need to tell Mom," I started, though I knew he did. Besides, I heard echoes of my classmates, telling me I hadn't needed to tell anyone about Trevor.

I reached out my arms to him. "Come here."

He shook his head. "Kevin's waiting to play computer games." Kevin had moved away two years ago, but he and Luke still played together using webcams.

"Go play," I said. "It's all good."

# CHAPTER 33

# July 11th and 12th: Nadia

Dad heard from Mom about my new beliefs, but he didn't seem to care. Nor did Chad, when he heard. His new girlfriend was a different story. She was very vocal when she and Chad came to visit next Friday evening.

Chad had recently started dating an evangelical Christian, Nadia. Nadia was one of those who believes that God demands worship in a very particular way. When he brought her for dinner with us we waited while she said her grace out loud.

"Bless this food, and the hands that have prepared it. Let it nourish us so that we might serve you. Guide us away from false paths. Clear our eyes. Protect Chad, his family and especially his sister Jessica, who has gone through so much this year. Bring her back onto your path, away from the false worship."

She finished her prayer and opened her eyes. We were all staring at her.

"Calm down, sis," Chad said as though I had already responded in anger.

"You don't mind?" Nadia said to me. "I only want the best for you. Chad's told me how hard this year has been to you."

Of course, I minded. What right had she to pray to God to change me? What right had she to judge me?

She continued speaking, "I know Chad will want to have all his family with him in heaven someday. I lived for years with a fear that my dad would die before he found Christ, and that he would be lost to me forever."

Afterwards, when I was calm, I could wonder how honest Chad had been to her about the rest of the family's religious beliefs. I doubt any of my family had "found Christ" in the way she was talking about. At the time though, I was trying to think how to defend myself. I knew though what was expected of me. I knew I had to make some self-deprecating comment to try to smooth things over, let everyone know that I wasn't taking it personally. I knew that if I got upset or angry, Chad would judge me for that too. It would be my fault because no matter how rude she had been, I could have chosen to not respond in anger.

It was Luke who saved me. Luke had saved me the trouble of replying. "I'm on the wrong path too," he announced. "I believe that God is a giant alien fattening us up to feed us to his gigantic sacred pigs."

Luke liked being the center of attention. He thought he was clever mentioning pigs, because Islam and Judaism forbid eating pork, and he could go on about how and why that was a sign we were all destined to be fed to pigs.

"I think we've heard enough about this," Mom said. "We're not going to get into criticizing any religion, or," she looked pointedly at Luke, "making fun of their beliefs. Now Nadia, perhaps you could tell us how you and Chad met?"

I stabbed at the peas on my plate, seeing how many I could spear onto my fork at a time. I didn't really care as much about how they had met as about how they were going to break up. I sat there imagining different possible futures, all involving Chad dumping her. Chad had lots of experiencing dumping girlfriends. It probably wouldn't be long before he dumped Nadia.

The next day I met up with Evelyn and recounted to her what had happened in the dinner with Nadia.

"I feel dirty," I said, "like by keeping the peace I was helping them degrade me, keeping quiet in the face of the rudeness. I shouldn't have to accept her comments and condescension."

"You didn't accept them. You knew they are a reflection of her, not you, and you chose to act so as to win what mattered to you at the time: peace. Other times you might choose differently. You might choose to fight."

"And then I'll be judged for that, and told that I'm too sensitive, and what should I expect when I choose strange unknown religious beliefs," I said.

"Yes, and then you'll get to choose again how you respond to those comments. But know that you aren't too sensitive. You're not too anything. You're you."

"I'm me, but that doesn't pre-empt the possibility of my

being too sensitive. People aren't perfect, but we shouldn't have to accept our imperfections completely, right? We can still work to improve?"

She sat quietly. I knew neither of us were really putting into words exactly what we wanted to say. We were skirting around the edges of our thoughts, trying to describe the impossible. Then she spoke.

"We can't try to improve, because what might seem like an improvement can be a fault in another way. We can try to change, to adapt better and make things easier for ourselves, or to better reflect the person we want to be."

I shook my head. "I can't fight," I said. "I won't be able to. There's something wrong inside of me, something that makes it so I can't say no, I can't fight, I can't defend myself at all. I ran away when school got too tough and I'll run away again. I don't know how to defend myself."

She was looking at me with such care and concern, but I didn't think she understood. Evelyn knew what she believed. She wasn't plagued with doubts and questions as I was. She didn't see five sides to every question, as I did. She could see what it was she wanted and stick to it, confident that the choice she made was right.

If it had been Evelyn at the dinner table and she had chosen to fight with Nadia it would have been because she knew her beliefs were worth defending. I hoped mine were, but feared they weren't. If it were Evelyn at the dinner table and she chose to stay quiet, it would be because she knew Nadia was not worth the effort. Either way, she would have made the decision she wanted to make.

People thought that because I told the truth at the trial, I had courage. The truth is I had been too scared to lie.

I wasn't even sure if I would have told the truth, if I had I known how angry people were going to be after. I might have risked lying.

I was weak and confused. I didn't fight Nadia because I didn't want to make a scene and because I feared my brother's disapproval, but I also kept quite because I wasn't entirely sure. I wanted to believe. I wanted to have faith, but I had doubts.

Nadia's opinion of my religion didn't matter. That I could concede I knew. But I still remembered Damian's comments about magic and religion being impossible things meant to give people false comfort. I'd never really let go of those thoughts. They were much more persuasive than Nadia's comments.

How could there be spirits, Gods or goddesses? How could thoughts matter? I took comfort from religion, but I could not defend it.

# July 13th: Sunday after church

Mom kept glancing at me as we walked to church the next morning. Did she think I was going to grow horns or be struck by lightning or something when I walked into the church? I had been attending church with the family anyway, despite my growing interest in Wicca. Sure, I missed weeks occasionally, but most of the time I went. What was she thinking? I hoped she wouldn't bring my religious beliefs up publicly. Would she try talking to the minister about me?

I tried not to worry. I tried to focus on Luke. He was walking next to Dad, just a few steps ahead of me and Mom. Unfortunately, their topic was computer games, and there was no way that was going to distract me from the strange silence with Mom.

"What are you thinking?" I asked, finally.

Mom's large hoop earrings swayed slightly as she turned to look at me. "I'm thinking about Mackenzie," she answered.

Her answer surprised me. Why would Mom think about Mackenzie? Had something happened to Mackenzie, that she knew about from the other mothers, that I had missed hearing about?

"Why?" I asked.

"Well, I thought you and she had started talking again, and maybe you might want to spend some more time with her again. Maybe you'd like to invite her over for supper. You and she used to spend so much time together."

"She's going to Vancouver for a couple of weeks," I said, still wondering why Mom was talking about her.

"All the more reason for you to invite her over sooner, rather than later," Mom said. We walked a few more steps in silence. She had something on her mind but seemed uncertain about whether to say it or not.

"I've been thinking," she said, "and I want you to hear me out before you react. It was Evelyn who introduced you to Wicca, right?"

I nodded. "Yes, but..." My shoulders and jaw tensed up as I prepared for the onslaught of unjust arguments.

"No, I'm not done yet," Mom said firmly. "I haven't made up my mind about Wicca yet, and I'm not upset with Evelyn for that. You're old enough to pick your own friends and I won't try to stop you from doing things with her. I'm grateful for how she's cheered you up after everything this spring. However, you've heard the saying not to keep all your eggs in one basket, right? Well, it might be good for you to not rely too strongly on just one friend. If, while you're learning about Wicca, you find there are things you are uncomfortable with, I don't want you to worry about losing your only friend over it. I want you to have other friends too. You and Mackenzie were good friends for a long time, and it wouldn't hurt to spend more time with her, would it?"

Her argument wasn't as unjust as I feared. I could handle it. I took a deep breath to continue calming myself. We were approaching the front steps of the church and there wasn't room for argument anyway.

Besides, it might be okay to see Mackenzie, if it were just her and I. I did miss her.

"Ok," I said.

I was still reflecting on what Mom said while the service started. She was being unfair to doubt Evelyn. Evelyn wasn't into anything scary. Her version of Wicca wasn't going to make me uncomfortable, though there had been things online about Wicca that did. We couldn't help there being stupid uncomfortable stuff online where anyone could write anything. After all, there were creepy Christian things online too.

How would religion get between us anyway? There had been one line in a ritual that Evelyn had sent me that had made me a little uncomfortable. The line had sexual connotations I hadn't liked, but that wasn't a big deal. We didn't include anything in our summer solstice ceremony that we hadn't both agreed on.

I shook my head, clearing away the thoughts. All was good. The next Wiccan holiday was coming up soon and we would have to get busy on planning that. What could we do for that? I payed little attention to the church service and focused on my plans.

When the service was over, I told Mom I was going to leave quickly myself, rather than wait out the coffee and visiting time. The way she pursed her lips and stared at me made me wonder again if she had plans to have me talk to Rev. Rickson right after church. I thought I knew what might prevent that.

"I'll stop off at Mackenzie's," I said. "I'll invite her for supper."

"Ok," Mom agreed.

"Can I go too?" Luke asked. He didn't want to hang around while Mom and Dad talked with others.

"Not this time," I said, and I started towards the door before anyone could argue. Behind me I could hear Luke start to whine and Mom sighing.

Luke caught up with me at the door. "Mom said I could walk home," he announced.

"You'll be by yourself," I said. "I'm not going home yet."

"I can do it," he said.

I thought he could. I could, when I was his age. It was tempting to think of him as younger than he was, because he got upset to easily and needed help calming down. However, he knew the way home and he could probably get there without running into something that would set him off. He'd be fine as long as no one talked to him.

It wasn't far to MacKenzie's house. It was a small brick building with a huge Manitoba maple-tree in the front yard. The tree's thick branches were bent low and made for good climbing. In the fall, the ground around it would be littered with its little winged seeds. We used to gather handfuls of them, climb up into the tree and then drop them slowly one by one watching them twirl as they fell. I scanned the ground for them as I walked up the driveway, but it wasn't the right season.

When Mackenzie opened the door I could see over her shoulder, through the living room and into the kitchen. The rest of her family – her brother, sister, and her mom – were at the table eating lunch.

"I'm sorry," I said. "I shouldn't have come over lunchtime."

"No, it's ok." She stepped forward onto the front steps and closed the door behind her. "What's up?" The concern was evident in her voice. I hadn't just dropped by in ages.

"I don't know. I wanted to invite you to come for supper." It felt incredibly formal saying that. We used to eat at each other's houses all the time, if our visits stretched too close to mealtimes, but I hadn't ever dropped by to invite her before.

"Oh... sure, ok."

"Ok, see you then," I said, starting down the front steps.

"I tried to call you, you know," she said. "After the fireworks. You were out."

"I went canoeing," I said, "with Evelyn and Damian."

She shrugged, her frizzy black hair bouncing as she did. "That's what Luke told me. I just wanted to apologize for Trevor and Destiny being jerks. They didn't mean it. Destiny had been really scared about losing Walnut. Trevor was showing off for Destiny because she's been going out with some guy from Edmonton."

It seemed so weird to hear her say that. It wasn't Destiny or Trevor's first time being jerks. It wasn't like they were nicer people other time. How did she not know that? I stood there, awkwardly, too stunned to reply.

Her apology irked me. It was claiming Trevor and Destiny

as part of her group, her friends. She was on their side, even when they were out of line. She was making excuses for them.

I took a deep breath; a lump formed in my throat.

"Ok, well..." I said, starting to turn away. I meant to say "see you at supper time" but the words didn't come out. It seemed easiest to just walk off, head home then try to explain how uncomfortable it made me to have her apologize. I went three or four steps. I heard the spring of her front door as she opened it.  Then I stopped.

"Mack," I said, turning around. She stood with the door open, waiting to see what I wanted.

I took a few steps towards her. She let the door shut.

"Mack, I can't. I try to not care. I try to not care what happened before and not hold you responsible for things others did but then you say something like that, and everything crumbles."

"I said what?" she asked, confused.

"You apologized for Trevor. You defend him. You apologize for him. You care about him. Despite all he's done, he's still part of your group. I thought maybe we could be friends again, but we can't. I can't, forget it."

I turned. She called after me, but I ran.

*Thump, thump, thump.* Every thump of my foot hitting the sidewalk brought me further from her house.

"Jessica," I heard her call again. "Jessica, that's not fair."

I didn't look back. I just ran.

I had tried to forgive her. I had wanted to forgive her, because I missed her, and I wanted things to be the same again. But I couldn't forgive her, not really, because the hurt wouldn't end. There'd be another time and then another where she'd be hanging out with them and I'd be excluded, and maybe I should be okay with that but I wasn't, because no matter how much she might act like she wanted to be friends again she was okay with them excluding me. Maybe it was unfair of me, because she was just one person and couldn't change the rest of them. But if she was willing to accept them being who they are and act like an apology was all it took to make up for it, then she wasn't someone I could be friends with.

Yet it felt hypocritical of me to reject Mackenzie and accept Joshua. He hadn't cut himself off from his other friends, yet somehow it didn't hurt as much. Was it because he was a guy and the idea of him having a group of guy friends seemed natural? Was it because he'd given up being so defensive of them and we'd just gotten on with life?

Even thinking the thoughts, "no, I don't want to see her" felt unfair and wrong of me. She had rejected me earlier because our other friends wouldn't be friends with her unless she did. Now I was doing the same thing, rejecting her because she wouldn't reject those other friends? I was unfairly trying to control her, wasn't I?

No, I was reacting out of pain. She had hurt me incredibly and continued to do so. I had tried to forgive everyone, but they were still going to be jerks to me, so I should be able to protect myself. Emotional self-defense, right?

Besides, no one has to be friends with anyone else. I didn't owe her anything, did I?

Mom would be annoyed, but oh well.

I didn't want to head home. I wanted to talk to Evelyn and

have her assurance that I wasn't being unfair, but if I went over to her house I'd be probably interrupting her lunch and I didn't want to create another scene, no matter how small. Instead I headed to the old barn. I could spend a bit of time there alone with my parents and Luke just assuming I had gotten caught up visiting at Mackenzie's house.

I didn't go into the barn. I sat cross-legged outside in the sun. I closed my eyes and tilted my head up towards the sun imagining the warmth of the sun like a god or goddesses love pouring down on me. I put my leaned back, putting my weight on my arms and letting my fingers dig down so that they could touch the cool soil buried under the dry grass. The sun and the soil felt good. I felt good.

I didn't feel deserving of any goodness. I had just hurt Mackenzie and disappointed my mom and who knows what else. I had probably annoyed Luke by not letting him walk home with me, and now who knows, I might be holding up their lunch. It was all minor things.

Minor things. Minor things counted for lots when I wondered if, at my core, I was wrong. In all the little decisions about when to forgive and when to hold a grudge and when to walk away, had I been wrong?

I uncrossed my legs and lay down on the grass. I was just an insignificant person sandwiched between the earth and the sky. I wasn't even a sandwich, more just a tiny bit of something caught between pieces of something greater.

Mom thought I was walking away from Christianity. Was it? Would it matter if I was? As I lay there on the grass I felt the presence of something greater. My mom would call it God and Evelyn would call is the Goddess. Damien, I knew, would say it was my imagination, and maybe that was okay. Maybe it was okay if I was imagining something greater than myself for a bit; something loving me while I wondered if I was unlovable.

I wouldn't always be able to forgive and I'd need boundaries. It would be ok, I think, if Evelyn and Damien were my only friends for a bit. Evelyn would leave for college or university. Maybe I'd join her at whatever university she decided to attend.

An image flashed into my mind of Evelyn at university, talking with others, laughing. I felt a momentary flash of jealousy. If I joined her a year later, would she still have room for me in her circle of friends, or would she too many new ones? For just a second or two, I could sympathize with Damien's sense of possessiveness and his dread of her leaving. Then I let go of that image. We would keep in touch. It would be enough.

I wanted to be strong, able to handle whatever came. For the moment, I felt like I might be able to.